D0394886

"Rest easy, children. Your world is about to implode."

DOUBLECROSS
MISSION TITANIC

THE 39 CLUES

JUDE WATSON

SCHOLASTIC INC.

For all the clue hunters on the message
boards — we couldn't do this without you!
— J.W.

Library of Congress Control Number: 2014953663

ISBN 978-0-545-74781-3

10 9 8 7 6 5 4 3 2 1   15 16 17 18 19/0

Cover images: ship and pieces by Freddie Bethune for Scholastic; gears © cherezoff/
Shutterstock and © stiven/Shutterstock; blueprint © amgun/Shutterstock; ship
blueprint © Hein Nouwens/Shutterstock; *Titanic* drawing by the-blueprints.com.
Interior images: vial page 10 © studioVin/Shutterstock; vial labels page 10,
smartphone page 145, and emei piercer page 170 by Charice Silverman for
Scholastic; ship page 145 by Freddie Bethune for Scholastic.
Book and cover design by Charice Silverman

First edition, March 2015

Printed in the U.S.A. 23

Scholastic US: 557 Broadway • New York, NY 10012
Scholastic Canada: 604 King Street West • Toronto, ON M5V 1E1
Scholastic New Zealand Limited: Private Bag 94407 • Greenmount, Manukau 2141
Scholastic UK Ltd.: Euston House • 24 Eversholt Street • London NW1 1DB

CHAPTER 1

Attleboro, Massachusetts

Revenge is sweet, but humiliation is sweeter.

And world domination is a definite plus.

He stood on the knoll overlooking the mansion. It had burned and it had been rebuilt — stronger, better. Just like him.

The children were inside, the ones who thought they knew what they were doing.

The undeserving.

His plan was in place. He would defeat them, *own* them. What they'd done to the Cahill family was unforgivable. Made the Cahills soft and stupid, vulnerable, open, a loose confederation of "family" instead of the dense, glittering network of brilliance and strength it should be. Exchanging ideas about how to *share* rather than *control* and *dominate*.

Grace, you would weep if you saw this. You were never

soft. You had that ruthless streak. Until the end, when your fear overcame your reason.

You gave it all away.

It had taken years of planning, but it was together now.

Rest easy, children. Your world is about to implode.

CHAPTER 2

First, there was Napoleon Bonaparte.

He set out to conquer the world and succeeded. Became a general at twenty-four. Crowned himself Emperor of France about ten years later. He did spectacularly well until that disaster at Waterloo, when the Brits beat the pants off him.

What happens when you surpass your role model?

Ian Kabra smiled as he climbed onto a step stool and faced the mirror. So much handsome stared back. It was almost too much. He smoothed back the lock of dark hair that kept falling in his eyes. Imperfection was just annoying.

At seventeen, he was head of the most powerful family in the world.

Plus, he was taller.

Take that, Cousin Napoleon!

Ian didn't think that genetics was destiny, but it was a definite plus having Napoleon in his family tree, as well as Catherine the Great, Benjamin

Franklin, and Winston Churchill. The greatest strategic minds in the history of civilization were all related in the twisting branches and tendrils of the Cahill family line. Even today, the real titans — giants of industry, technology, finance, art, music, athletics, endurance — were all related to him, from Nobel Prize–winning scientists to Edith Laverne Oh-Flurrie of Norman, Oklahoma, who patented a new sewing machine bobbin at the age of ninety-two and treated herself to a new armchair recliner on the proceeds. Which were somewhere in the neighborhood of fifty million dollars.

Edith was an Ekat, the branch of the Cahills that was studded with science and technology geniuses. The Tomas were exceptional physical specimens. The Janus, the creatives, were the artists and dreamers who set the world on fire. Ian's own branch, the Lucians, were, like Cousin Napoleon, brilliant strategists and thinkers. And then there were the Madrigals, the under-the-radar branch that had come out of hiding only recently. Ian had been born a Lucian (thank goodness — Ian still felt a deep loyalty to them), but was a Madrigal as well. The Madrigals were now the leaders of the Cahills because they were the only branch the others agreed to trust.

Yes, the Cahills were exceptional, but they needed someone to lead them. Enter Ian Kabra.

From a control panel by his bed he could activate screens that would put him in touch with Cahill family leaders all over the world. He could put the entire mansion on lockdown, order people to do what *he* planned and strategized, and request his morning tea.

"You sure you want another quarter inch, bud? Seems kinda short." The tailor stood in the master closet, squinting at Ian's trouser legs.

From his position on the step stool, Ian frowned down at the tailor. "Mr. Funicello, I gave you precise measurements from my London tailor. And you delivered trousers that were an inch and one half too long. There is no mistake whatsoever." He gestured at his suit. "This must be done right. I have an important meeting in a week."

"So you said already. Three times." The tailor set out his box of materials and, sighing heavily, bent over to fold Ian's trouser hem.

What Americans didn't know about tailoring! Trousers should be a precise length. What was hard about that? A graceful curve on the shoe, not cascading like a waterfall around your ankles. His cousin Jonah Wizard's trousers? *Painful* to look upon.

Living in the United States after London . . . well, it had its challenges. You had to put up with the horrors of tea bags, for one thing. And he was constantly having to *explain* things. How when he told the driver to put his suitcase in the boot, the driver just stared at him. As if *trunk* made any more sense than *boot*? And when at the cinema (twenty films in one theater!

Now there's a concept!) he suggested to his cousin Hamilton Holt that they try the lift instead of the crowded escalator, Hamilton had lifted him in his arms and carried him up the stairs. Humiliating! As a Tomas, his cousin had an impressive physique, but surely even Hamilton's brain could grasp the British term for "elevator."

He was homesick for London, for fog, real marmalade, and people who understood hand-tailoring and the class system. People who knew how important his family was, even though he had disowned them. Only his father was left, and Ian was perfectly happy never to see him again.

Raised by vicious snobs, it was true. But snobs with money and style.

Ian admired his suit, appreciating the mirrors that gave him a total view of his appearance. He'd had to install them when he'd moved into the master bedroom. He'd created a secret safe room and taken the opportunity to expand the closet. As the former head of the family, his cousin Amy Cahill had supervised the renovation of the half-destroyed mansion, but a girl who lived in gray T-shirts and blue jeans did not understand the importance of walk-in closets.

A week from now, Ian would lead his first annual Cahill Family Summit meeting. Branch leaders from all over the world would attend on videoconference, and notable Cahills would stream into Grace Cahill's mansion. Every detail had to be right, from the scones and clotted cream of the elaborate English tea to the technical challenges of screens and cables and the smooth operation of the *Gideon*, the Cahill family's own satellite.

Not just right, Ian amended, his gaze unfocused as the tailor measured his inseam. *Lockstep perfect.*

Because lately, just in the past few weeks, things had seemed a bit . . . wobbly.

From the very beginning, the squabbling Cahills had been hard to manage. He hadn't given Amy enough credit. She'd been a powerhouse in an ill-fitting T-shirt, and everyone had looked up to her. They'd known that she and her brother had defeated Cahill enemies and fashioned the family into an organized unit. It had been her vision that had rebuilt the mansion, had pushed the technology for the satellite, had brought everyone together for conferences and retreats, had tightened the digital network. How she'd gotten them to agree, and to agree to disagree, he still didn't know.

He thought it would be *fun* to give orders. He didn't expect people to question his decisions! The truth was, he thought he'd be a far superior leader to Amy. And he *was*, in many ways, of course . . . but why did the family seem to be slipping from his grasp? Branch leaders not checking in, prominent Cahills not taking his calls . . . the *egos* he had to deal with . . .

The tailor had finished marking the hem. He laid out a row of pins.

"Be sure it's straight."

"Sure, bud."

"I am not your *bud*, Mr. Funicello. Are you aware of who pays your bill?"

Cara Pierce burst into the room, breathless. "Ian!"

Ian grabbed at his trousers. He wasn't wearing a belt, and he wasn't entirely sure all his seams were sewn. "Cara! Did you ever hear of a quaint custom called knocking?"

"Oh, please, I knew your tailor was here."

"Precisely!"

"Listen, Your Highfalutingness, we've got a problem."

Cara strode toward him, impossibly beautiful and incredibly annoying. As a matter of fact, *impossible* and *incredible* basically defined his second-in-command. Cara made fun of him constantly, wore a baseball cap in the house, ate potato chips from a can, and could probably beat him up. She was also most likely smarter than he was. She was definitely, absolutely, completely not his type.

Except . . . she was his soul mate. She was his one true pairing. She was the sugar in his cup of tea, the butter on his crumpets, the tinsel on his tree. His destiny.

She just didn't know it yet.

She raked a hand through her chin-length blond hair and held up her smartphone. "I'm having problems logging in to *Gideon*."

"Atmospheric disturbance?"

"Could be. But why is the Cahill Summit on my calendar for today?"

He turned back to the mirror. "Don't fret, it's next week."

"If you can tear yourself away from yourself, take a look at your phone."

"Can't you see I'm in the middle of something important? OW!"

"Sorry, bud."

"You stuck me!"

"Ian, *look at your phone*!"

He gave in and fished his phone out of his jacket pocket. He frowned. "It does say today. Must be a software glitch. Isn't that your area? You're the master hacker."

"It's not a glitch; it was *moved*," Cara said. "Just a few minutes ago. The meeting is now scheduled to take place in five minutes!"

"Well, maybe on our phones, but not in actuality."

"Well, *in actuality*, I can no longer log on to *Gideon* to check the network. This feels hinky."

"*Hinky?* What sort of word is that? If you keep using slang, I'm going to have to start watching American television, and nobody wants that. I can't make a decision based on emotion. Tell me an observable fact, and—"

Maybe he'd gone too far. Because suddenly Cara's beautiful clear green eyes had turned icy and she was coming at him hard. Feet first.

CHAPTER 3

The kick missed him by a millimeter and connected with Mr. Funicello's chin. The skinny tailor went flying. His head slammed back against the wall and he went limp.

"Cara! I admit the fellow couldn't sew a straight seam, but—"

Cara bent down and picked up a vial that had rolled across the carpet. "The pins." She gestured at the mirror. "I saw him dip them into this liquid."

"So he wasn't just clumsy," Ian said. He put out a hand to steady himself.

"How many times did he stick you?"

"Just once."

"How do you feel?"

"Uh. Surprised? Irritated? Gobsmacked?"

"Any numbness?" she asked urgently. "Pain?"

"I feel absolutely topping, except for the part where you're making me extremely nervous."

Cara squinted at the label and then typed it into her phone. "Okay," she said after a few seconds that felt like hours. "It's not poison."

"Excellent news." Ian tried not to look relieved. It was important to keep his cool in front of Cara. He had a feeling she didn't appreciate his manly qualities.

"It's a mild sedative. The cumulative effect wouldn't even have knocked you out. Just slowed you down. He had a handful of pins, so he was planning to scratch you plenty of times." Cara tossed the bottle into the bag and stood, her hands on her hips. "Do me a favor. The next time I tell you something's wrong, try believing it."

"You hardly conveyed a sense of great urgency," Ian said.

"What do I have to do, kick you?"

"You almost did!"

"Sorry I missed," Cara muttered.

Ian bent down to rifle through the tailor's pockets. "No ID. Just in case he got caught, he'd want to be untraceable. Mr. Berman did the background check. We can get information from him. But why would someone want to sedate me?" Ian's mind clicked over possibilities. "A kidnapping? Not again!"

"Well, that's straight from the Cahill playbook, but I don't think so. What was that?"

The sound of tires on the brick-paved courtyard came to them. They heard the slam of a car door. Cara hurried to the double-height windows and peered outside into the gray winter morning.

"There are fifteen limousines in our courtyard and a line of cars stretching back to the gate," she said. "Is that enough *actuality* for you? This wasn't a glitch in our calendars. Somebody rescheduled this meeting! They didn't want to kidnap you—"

"—they just wanted to slow me down," Ian said. "The question is who. And why."

"You could cancel the meeting."

Ian shook his head. "Impossible. They're here! They'd never stand for that."

"You could be walking into a trap."

"It's not a trap if I see what's coming."

They dragged Mr. Funicello—or whoever he really was—into the safe room and locked the door. As they hurried down the wide, carpeted stairs, Ian and Cara could hear the murmur of voices growing louder. At the landing overlooking the grand entrance hall, they bumped into a frazzled Mr. Berman running upstairs toward them.

"Mr. Kabra, Ms. Pierce—why didn't you tell me the

meeting was today? There are cars arriving! The Cahill family leaders! Governors! Ambassadors! Astronauts! Nobel Prize winners! Olympic athletes! Somebody parachuted into the meadow! There's a Buddhist monk down there! And they'll all need coffee, and tea, and whatever the Russian ambassador drinks. I shall have to prepare a *lunch*! I can't just make crab soufflé out of thin air, you know!"

"Relax, Mr. Berman," Cara said. "Just do the best you can."

Mr. Berman looked at Ian. "Are you all right, sir? You look . . . pale."

"I'm fine. But Mr. Funicello is enjoying a short stay in our safe room," Ian said, trying to tuck his shirt more securely in his pants.

"Should I . . ."

"He'll be all right. Let's stay focused. We need to greet our guests."

Mr. Berman straightened. "Yes, sir. I won't fail you." He turned and hurried down the stairs.

Good old Berman. Ian surveyed the hall below. It was packed with his relatives, close and distant.

And at least one enemy.

Cahills could be ruthless when it came to personal agendas. Someone had a vested interest in Ian not being on top of his game.

"Hamilton and Nellie aren't here," Cara said. "All our allies must still think the meeting is next week!"

"It's all right." Ian focused on the faces in the crowd, planning his strategy. "Just make sure all the remote feeds are working."

"I'm not worried about the *feeds*. I'm worried about whoever targeted you being in the house right now. I'm hitting the emergency signal."

Ian shook his head. "Not necessary. I've got this." If he couldn't handle a little sabotage, what kind of a leader was he?

"It was an attack on home ground. It's protocol."

"Don't alert anyone. That's an order."

Something cool and distant arose in Cara's gaze. Ian had seen it before. She didn't like orders, and she didn't like being reminded that technically, he was the boss. He'd put his foot in it again, had blundered when he'd meant to be strong. But there was no time to fix it. Ian continued down the stairs.

He looked over the sea of heads and cleared his throat. Gradually, the buzz died down.

"Welcome to the Cahill mansion," he said. "I am delighted to see all of you."

A gray streak crashed into his vision. The cat leaped through the air and landed on Ian's shoulder, a move the demented, *evil* creature enjoyed. Ian had always hated Saladin. He'd never imagined that with Amy and Dan's departure he'd end up inheriting the catmonster.

He swatted Saladin off just as Cara lunged to grab

him. Saladin evaded Cara's reaching hands and slid down Ian's trouser leg, using his claws.

Ian heard the sound of seams ripping. He grabbed for his waistband, but it was too late.

He stood before the assembled mass of the most important Cahills in the world in his boxer shorts.

CHAPTER 4

Television studio, Glorious Kitchen cable network,
New York City

The smiling host faced the camera while the audience cheered.

"Welcome back to the finals of the home cooking contest! The winner will receive a profile in *Glorious Kitchen* magazine, plus a chance to be the host of his or her own cooking show! The judges have tasted some phenomenal food. Now, let's move on to our last finalist. Welcome, NELLIE GOMEZ!"

Wild cheers erupted. Nellie Gomez felt the waves of love pulsating from the audience. These were her people. Food people. She had introduced herself a week ago by saying "I love to eat. I love to cook. I once ate a fried grasshopper. My parents are totally pissed off I'm not at college right now." From that moment, she'd been their favorite.

This was her big break. Her own cooking show! She knew she could do it. She had saved her best recipe for last: her spicy crab cake soft tacos with lime yogurt sauce and mango salsa. Nobody had ever put crab cakes in a taco before, and it was genius. Her boyfriend, Sammy Mourad, had flipped over them. Her secret ingredient? Toasted pumpkin seeds.

And charm. Loads and loads of charm.

Nellie set to work chopping and mixing, keeping up a steady chatter that had the audience laughing and clapping. She handed her plate of pure, fresh deliciousness to the judges.

She could tell by their faces that the tacos were a hit. One judge's eyes closed and he almost fell off his chair.

The judges leaned over to confer. Nellie's nerves were now at a screaming point.

She felt her cell phone buzz in her apron pocket. Three quick bursts. The Cahill emergency alert. She drifted back behind the counter and gave it a quick look. Her face flushed.

"And now for the winner of our *Glorious Kitchen Home Cook Competition*! The judges have reached a verdict!"

The spotlight ranged over the hopeful faces of the contenders.

"NELLIE GOMEZ!"

Pandemonium reigned as the audience stamped and howled.

The spotlight roamed, hitting the losing contenders, searching, wavering . . .

Nellie Gomez was gone.

CHAPTER 5

Paris, France

The crowds had been gathering since daybreak. International movie star Jonah Wizard's latest blockbuster film, *Quick Exit*, was having its European premiere. Fans crammed the bleachers. Signs waved: JONAH WIZARD EST FORMIDABLE! JE T'AIME JONAH!

Photographers clicked and jockeyed for position as the costars arrived, one after the other.

"I could use a burger," Jonah said. He gazed out at the crowd from the backseat of an SUV parked across the street.

"Get Mr. Wizard a burger," a thin, tense woman said to a tall, muscular guy in jeans and an I BRAKE FOR STOP SIGNS T-shirt.

"Dude, I'm his bodyguard, not his maid," Hamilton Holt said in a genial tone. He had signed up for the tour to watch his best friend's back, not wait on him. It was his first movie tour, and he was constantly floored by how Jonah's every wish was granted. *A glass of water, Mr. Wizard? Certainly. Still or sparkling? Ice or lukewarm? Lemon or lime? French or Italian?* When Hamilton had added, *Bathroom or kitchen?* Jonah had cracked up. The publicist—what was her name? Mandy? Sandy? Andy?—had not.

"I can wait," Jonah added. "It's just that I've been in interviews all day. I'm tired of cheese. They keep giving me cheese."

The publicist whipped out her phone and spoke into it in dire tones. *"No more cheese for Mr. Wizard."*

There was a knock at the window. It was time to go. The fans had been whipped up into the appropriate frenzy. The photographers were primed and waiting. Hamilton slipped into his leather jacket, the one that Jonah insisted he buy so he'd look like a kick-butt bodyguard.

"Ready, dude?" Jonah asked Ham.

"Ready, bro."

They exchanged a grin. Celebrities had a habit of complaining about premieres and adoring crowds, but nobody was having a better time than Jonah and Ham. Hotel suites, a private plane, free fruit! Awesome.

No one had been more surprised than Ham when he'd become best friends with his famous distant Cahill cousin. Jonah was his polar opposite. He'd been a hip-hop star at thirteen, a legend at sixteen, and was now a movie star. He had enough electricity to power the City of Light. He was a Janus, the branch of the Cahills that was all about creativity and charisma.

Ham was a Tomas—an athlete with a fondness for sweat and electrolytes.

Ham exited first. He held the door for Jonah, who emerged with his publicist and started across the street. Ham followed, his eyes constantly moving behind his dark glasses, tracking every shift and turn, making sure nobody was breaking through the barriers and heading for them. Jonah and Ham had been through a lot together—almost died together on a mountain in the Bavarian Alps—so this was easy stuff. All he had to do was watch out for paparazzi.

Jonah adopted the rolling, supercasual walk he favored when cameras were clicking. He waved at the crowd. Ham kept close but allowed a sight line for cameras.

Jonah was stopped by a pretty journalist in a trim velvet coat.

"Meester Weezhard, 'ow do you feel about premiering your film in Paris?"

"I'm living the dream," Jonah said. "My favorite city!"

"And 'ow do you think French girls compare to Americans?"

Hamilton felt his phone vibrate in his jacket pocket. Three short bursts.

Emergency signal.

He could tell by Jonah's face that he'd felt it, too.

"One speaks French, the other speaks English," Jonah said. He ended this nonsensical sentence with a chuckle of such dazzling charm that the reporter laughed and the audience applauded.

Ham followed Jonah as he brushed by the microphones and photographers and made a beeline for the theater. The publicist tripped after them on high heels, trying to catch up.

"There's an exit down the right-side aisle," Ham said. He'd already checked out the theater. Part of the job. "Leads into an alley. Metro station two blocks away."

"Mr. Wizard! Mr. Wizard! Your seat is in the third row! On the left! Not that way! Hello? Bodyguard, whatever your name is? You're supposed to *hover*, not talk to the talent!" She caught up to them and leaned into Jonah. "You have to take your seat! You're sitting next to the ambassador!" she hissed.

"Sorry, Sandy," Jonah said. "Gotta breeze."

CHAPTER 6

Attleboro, Massachusetts

Ian felt perspiration slip down between his shoulder blades. He *never* perspired under pressure.

It was hard to regain your authority once everyone had seen you in your underwear.

He had changed at lightning speed and now moved through the room, speaking a few words here and there, trying to connect with as many notables as he could, trying to pick up clues as to who was out to sabotage him. An overly warm greeting could be just as telling as a brush-off.

Ian had already spotted Magnus Hansen, the new head of the Tomas. Whenever Ian headed for him, it seemed as though Magnus was suddenly on the other side of the room.

Back in the 1990s, Magnus had won four Olympic gold medals in downhill skiing and smashed all speed records, and he was still a formidable athlete and a commanding presence. Tall, blond, incredibly fit in a navy sweater and blazer, he moved through the room as though he were the host, shaking hands and clapping backs. Ian had been surprised when Magnus had taken over the leadership of the Tomas. He had dropped out of sight for years. There had been talk that he'd been asked to leave after some kind of financial trouble with the Tomas treasury. Things must have been cleared up. Ian made a mental note to discover the details.

He watched as Magnus kissed Patricia Oh on both cheeks. She was the grandniece of Bae Oh, the former head of the Ekats, who was now in prison. She had never gotten involved with the Cahill family much. Her home was in Singapore, and she lived to shop and go out to lunch. Word was that Bae had given her a large allowance to stay out of his hair.

Then suddenly, this year she had become the Ekat branch leader.

He watched Patricia as she touched Magnus's arm and said something in his ear. She seemed to sense Ian's eyes on her and flicked a glance at him. He smiled and nodded. Her nod was cool as she moved away through the crowd.

Were they avoiding him?

Mr. Berman appeared at the staircase. He struck a small gong three times. "Ladies and gentlemen, please proceed to the library," he intoned.

Ian walked down the grand hallway, already rehearsing his first line. *Welcome, fellow Cahills. The spirit of Grace Cahill guides us as we meet in her beloved library. . . .*

He had foiled an attack once today. He was prepared to hit back when challenged. His enemy would be expecting him to be slow. He or she would be thinking Ian would be at half power, and he'd be dialed up to ten.

What was it that Hamilton always said? *Bring it.*

He waited until silence fell, and pressed a button. The black screens that hung on every wall blazed to life. Cahill leaders from all over the world appeared: from India, Russia, Norway, Kenya, Morocco, New Zealand, Manila . . .

And Cumbria, England. Ian gave a start. What was his father, Vikram Kabra, doing on-screen? Sure, he was a major Lucian, but ever since Ian's mother, Isabel, had been disgraced and died, Vikram had been in seclusion, unavailable to everyone, including his own son. Which didn't make that much of a difference, Ian thought, the tang of bitterness twisting his mouth. He was surprised he'd noticed at all. His father had only existed in his life to criticize and blame.

"Welcome, fellow Cahills," he began. "The spirit of Grace—"

Suddenly, it was like someone had thrown a blanket over his head. The lights went out. Everyone sat politely, thinking it was planned.

It wasn't.

Ian stabbed at the panel. Nothing happened. His power had been cut! The only illumination in the room was the faint bluish light from the screens as the Cahill notables waited.

Ian jumped as the screen blazed to life and a voice boomed out of the speakers.

"Good morning!"

On the screen directly behind him, an old man was smiling out at the audience. His face was smooth and tight, his teeth white and perfect, but Ian guessed he must have been in his eighties. He could pick out the telltale evidence of a good plastic surgeon better than anyone—his mother had been addicted to nips and tucks.

"Welcome, fellow Cahills."

That's my line! Ian twisted back, still stabbing at his panel. He searched the room for Cara.

"The spirit of Grace Cahill guides us as we meet in her beloved library. I am the Outcast. Sit back. I have a few things to say."

CHAPTER 7

The room was eerily quiet. Everyone was riveted to the man on the screen.

"Who am I? One of you." The Outcast leaned forward. His power didn't come from his erect posture; his big, gnarled hands; or his intense stare. It was something else, and Ian recognized it because he'd grown up with it. It was the ease of a man who knows he's the one with the ace in his pocket.

"I left the Cahills for a spell." He knitted his hands together. "I had to come back, just to ask one question."

"Excuse me!" Ian shouted, but he was drowned out by the thundering voice.

"Why are you letting children lead you?"

Ian spotted Cara at the back of the room. He whipped his finger across his throat, telling her to cut the power. She waved frantically as if to say, *I tried!*

Now that his eyes had adjusted, Ian quickly scanned the room. A Lucian was trained to read power shifts like surfers could read waves.

Read facial expressions and postures, notice glances. . . . Look for the people who are relaxed, not tense, because they knew this would happen. . . .

Foreboding hit him like repeated blows from a hammer.

The first two rows . . . sitting straight, not looking at each other, not puzzled. Just waiting.

Patricia Oh. Magnus Hansen. Someone he didn't recognize, a dark-haired, handsome man in his forties. He was keeping his head turned away slightly, and he wore tinted glasses. And was that man in black-framed round glasses Toby Griffon, the renowned architect? Next to him sat Melinda Toth, the Lucian billionaire businesswoman.

And sprinkled around the room . . . others, too. They *knew* this guy.

And his father. Still on screen. Vikram Kabra leaned back in his chair, as if he were lounging. Ian noted the sharp glint in his dark eyes. This was an ambush, and his father was part of it.

Ian felt the surprise of hot tears behind his eyes. He was suddenly seven years old again. He thought of the times he'd run to his father for comfort. Before he'd learned not to. *Young man, there is no need for sniffles. If you bleed, don't look for sympathy. Get yourself a handkerchief and get on with it.*

"We have placed our destiny in the hands of amateurs!" the Outcast boomed. "Grace used to say, *If your best instincts are your worst enemies, take your hands off the controls. Find someone else to fly the plane.*" The Outcast clasped his hands together. "Grace believed in family, but she didn't suffer fools. In this very room, Grace issued a challenge for a hunt for thirty-nine clues. The challenge was won by *her own grand-children.*" He held up a hand. "I'm not here to suggest that there could have been double-dealing, even though it seems remarkable that children could win over the best minds, bodies, skills, and leadership of branch leaders."

A murmur ran through the room. Ian saw some heads nodding.

"STOP!" Ian yelled.

"Let him speak!" Patricia Oh called. "He is making a great deal of sense."

"The clue hunt was a sham! Because of it, we allowed the young, the untried to lead us! First Amy and Dan Cahill, until they got bored and walked away. And now their friend, a pampered boy!"

The hairs stood up on Ian's neck as he heard the sound of his father's chuckle. That always meant a bit of cruelty was coming.

"I hear our bold leader made great changes. He added mirrors to the master suite," Vikram Kabra said.

Ian heard laughter ripple through the room. His face burned.

"This is insanity, my friends!" the Outcast cried. "We need to take our family back. It's time for some-one else to fly the plane."

"What are you suggesting, sir?" Ian shouted, trying to match the Outcast's volume and strength.

The Outcast smiled. It was a chilling smile, as though Ian had walked right into a trap. And he had. An amateur's mistake. He had asked a question that he didn't know the answer to.

"I'm so very glad you asked. I propose a test for current leadership."

"Yes!" Toby Griffon agreed. "What do you have in mind?"

Ian stared at him. *You already know what he's going to say. So does Magnus. And Patricia, and my father, and Melinda Toth. It's written all over your faces.*

"We are behind many of history's greatest triumphs," the Outcast said. "But we are also behind some of the biggest disasters. I've chosen four of them to replicate."

The room was now completely still. Ian swallowed. His eyes raked the room, looking for allies. No one would meet his glance. They were all fascinated by the Outcast. Hanging on his every word.

"And since children are so fond of riddles, we'll start with one each time. Ready?

"Your first disaster took place at sea
It was sad — rich and poor died in agony
Broke all records for calamity
For those still clad in pajamity
A collision caused the terrible losses

29

In the Maritimes you'll find the crosses
On Mont Blanc rest the ones to blame
Oh, to maim, blind, and kill, and have no shame!
It will happen again if you can't stop it
At least the Cahill fam will profit!"

His smile glittered with menace. "Cahill leadership has five days to guess the disaster and prevent it. No outsiders. If outsiders are brought in or consulted, the deal is off, the disasters take place, and the blood is on your hands."

"You're crazy," Ian said. No one heard him. "He's crazy!" he shouted. Couldn't they see the madness glittering in the man's eyes?

"I'm a fair man," the Outcast continued, as if Ian hadn't spoken. "So I'll give you until sunrise tomorrow to start the clock. Ready, set, go!"

The screen went black.

The lights blazed on.

"All right, everybody," Ian said. "Let's calm down. The first step is to discover the identity of that madman."

But no one was listening. They were talking anxiously, buzzing with concern and questions and statements.

Nobody was talking to him.

"Fellow Cahills!"

"I think we've had enough of you," Magnus said, standing.

As if responding to a signal, the entire first row of Cahills stood. They moved forward. Before he quite knew what was happening, Ian realized that they were flanking him and Cara. On either side of them were athletes from the Tomas branch, all lean, coiled muscle. One woman was famous for swimming the Bering Sea, and there was at least one pro football player who blocked the rest of the Cahills from interfering.

"Just a minute here—" Ian started, but they force-marched him out of the room.

"Hands off!" Cara shrugged off one of the men who had taken her elbow.

"This is a coup!" Ian shouted. He cast one desperate glance back, but the rest of the Cahills either seemed frozen . . . or were part of the conspiracy.

They marched Ian and Cara down the hallway to the front door. The cold February wind knifed through the doorway as Magnus flung it open.

"Mr. Berman!" Ian shouted. "Help us!"

He hung on to the doorframe, even though he knew it was undignified. "MR. BERMAN!"

But Mr. Berman was probably frantically making tea and sandwiches. The pro football player picked him up like kindling wood.

"You can either walk, or I'll throw you out," he said.

Cara's face was pale, but she tossed her hair and strolled out the door. "Come on, Ian," she said in a cool tone. "There are better ways to fight."

Ian gazed into the iceberg eyes of Magnus Hansen.

"Throw him out anyway," Hansen said. "He needs a lesson."

The next thing Ian knew, he was flying through the air. He landed hard on Grace's slate walkway. The shock of the landing rattled his bones. Tears sprang to his eyes from the pain.

"Anybody got a tissue?" Magnus laughed. "Wipe your nose, crybaby. Grace's house belongs to the grown-ups now."

CHAPTER 8

Chamonix, France

Against the startlingly clear blue sky, the snowy peaks of the Alps were a jagged line of majesty. Thousands of feet below, farms seemed scattered like an impatient toddler's toys.

It could be her last sight on earth.

Amy Cahill looked down at her feet, just an inch away from the edge. She felt the cold wind against her face, and she closed her eyes for just one second to gather her nerve. Then she dove off the side of the mountain.

The roar of the wind filled her ears, and her stomach dropped. The breath seemed ripped from her body, but she found enough to scream.

Every nerve in her body was alive and tingling. She hurtled through the air, conscious that any sudden move could endanger her flight and send her crashing into the face of the mountain. There was nothing to grab on to, nothing to break her fall. Just air.

Just thin air, and she was diving through it in a bright orange wingsuit that made her look like a flying squirrel.

Turning her head slightly, she caught sight of her brother. Behind the windscreen on his helmet, Dan was grinning. Her thirteen-year-old brother definitely enjoyed adrenaline.

She angled her body to slow her descent. She was hurtling down at a velocity of about eighty miles an hour, arms bent, shoulders strong, legs straight out behind her.

In less than a minute she had to curve around the mountain. This was the tricky part. Flying consisted of thousands of microadjustments. Birds made it look easy.

She took a breath and let it out slowly, staying loose. She didn't want to do what skydivers call "potato chipping" — keeping your muscles so tense that your body shudders its way through the descent. Any bit of instability could lead to an overcorrection. She was experienced at this sport by now, but if you weren't aware at all times of the things that could go wrong, you were stupid.

She remembered the words of her instructor. *Keep your airflow clean. Get comfortable in that suit. Wear it like your pj's. Don't concentrate on the valley floor. Your speed can fool you into thinking you're higher than you are. You don't want to end up like jam on the mountainside.*

She curved around the cliff face. Her ears were filled with the rush and roar of wind and the flapping of the edges of her suit. The valley spread below her, snowy and still. She spotted the bright orange wind-sock that marked the meadow landing site. It had been cleared of snow. It felt amazing to know that she could hit that tiny mark and land.

Gauging her speed and direction, she angled to the right. She hated for the ride to end.

Something caught the sun over her right shoulder. A helicopter. Amy felt a jolt of alarm that she immediately tamped down. Probably some billionaire heading to his ski chalet. Nothing to worry about.

The helicopter didn't turn.

It tilted, the sun glaring off the bubble of the windshield. Didn't it see them?

Amy angled away again. Dan was behind her. She wished she could see him, but turning that much would send her into a spin.

She could feel the percussion of the whirling blades in her chest. The copter was awfully close. Too close! Still coming fast, angling above her now . . .

"DAN!" she screamed, but of course he couldn't hear her over the wind in his ears.

She had only seconds now before she had to pull her pilot chute. Then she would be a sitting duck, vulnerable, tethered to the canopy.

She saw someone leap out of the open door of

the copter. He was free falling just yards away. This wasn't right! He was angling his body to come close to her.

Panic burst through her. She had to engage the canopy. At least she could control her descent, aim away from the attacker.

The chute deployed, and she felt the jerk and drag. The attacker was behind her now. He must have pulled his canopy, too.

They would land in the same meadow. And by the looks of that black helicopter, it would, too. This didn't make sense. It had to be an attack.

She made a perfect landing, barely kissing the ground. She fumbled with her harness, making sure that Dan was safely down as she ripped it off and threw off her helmet. She raced toward the intruder, planning the attack as she ran. She knew from experience that thugs usually didn't expect a sixteen-year-old girl to be a warrior. She needed to kick first, while he was still attached to his chute. Hampered by her wingsuit, Amy would never be able to get off a perfect blow to the windpipe.

But that didn't mean she wouldn't try.

She'd need to go airborne. She rotated, gathering speed, lifted off, her booted feet together and aiming for the only vulnerable space she could see—his neck—while he shouted and dodged.

How weird. It sounded like he was yelling *AMYYYYY*.

Amy clumsily connected with her attacker's shoulder,

and the impact spun her off balance. She fell on top of him and raised a fist. A strong hand gripped her wrist, blocking her.

Amy stared into familiar friendly eyes.

"Don't kill me, dude," her cousin Hamilton Holt said. "I come in peace."

CHAPTER 9

Dan raced awkwardly toward his sister in his wing-suit, laughing and trying to scramble out of it as he ran. "That was awesome!" he shouted over the noise of the copter as it banked and circled. "I always wondered if you could bring Ham down!"

Amy struggled to her feet. "Ham, are you crazy? I almost got killed! Who surprises someone when they're BASE jumping?"

"I thought you'd recognize me," Ham said, still lying on the ground.

"In midair? When you're wearing goggles and a helmet? While I'm falling *eighty miles an hour*?"

"I guess we didn't think it through," Ham said sheepishly. "We just wanted to be sure we could talk to you. You're not that easy to track down, you know!"

"We?" Dan felt a spurt of pleasure. He missed his friends. If Hamilton was here, Jonah couldn't be far behind. His peeps were here!

For the past six months, ever since they'd saved the world from World War III and walked away from the Cahill family, Dan and Amy had been in happy exile. They'd changed their last name to Swift—the birds that, according to legend, never land—and set their feet on a new, aimless path. With Grace's house in Ireland as their base, they'd wandered from country to country, to beaches and gardens and parks and cities, absorbing and looking. It had been six months of extended chill time, and it had been fun. Dan had felt the buzz of anxiety in his head slowly drain like a battery. He was the only one in the world who knew the formula for the Cahill family serum— the source of the Cahills' power. A substance that had the potential to make someone the most power-ful person in the world, if it didn't kill him or her first. That knowledge had haunted him once. Now he still carried it, but it didn't weigh him down any longer.

His hyperorganized sister had planned their wan-derings. She hired tutors and guides so that they kept up with schoolwork. They didn't want to be hermits— they checked in with their Uncle Fiske and their friends and family through video chats—but they didn't want to get involved with Cahill family business.

Amy frowned. "What's wrong? Is everyone okay?" she asked. "Fiske . . ."

"Everyone's okay," Hamilton said quickly. "But something happened."

The helicopter landed, its blades whirring. Ian scrambled out and hesitated, his hand on the door.

Dan felt his heart sink. This wasn't going to be pals hanging out. This was official Cahill family business. He exchanged a glance with his sister. They'd always been able to say a lot without talking. He felt the same reluctance in her, the same dread.

Whatever was aboard that copter, it was bad news. And they were both reluctant to greet it. They knew exactly how seriously bad Cahill news could get.

"I'll let Ian fill you in," Hamilton said. "C'mon."

The copter's blades were spinning to a stop as Cara exited and stood next to Ian. They were exactly the same height and a study in contrasts. Ian's dark skin and hair and elegant cashmere overcoat made him look like he stepped off a fashion runway. Cara was dressed in a jumpsuit, a fedora crammed on her head, and her hands in the pockets of a battered leather jacket. It was only recently that she'd been folded into the Cahill inner circle, and Dan thought that having one of the world's best computer security experts in your corner was just about the coolest thing ever.

Jonah jumped out of the copter, making it look like a dance move. He bumped fists with Dan.

"Reunited and it feels so good," he said.

"Terribly sorry about the unconventional summons." Ian scanned the mountains around them casually, as though he were a tourist admiring the view. "Natalie and I used to ski in Chamonix during school breaks. It was always a favorite spot of ours. A bit overrun with tourists, of course . . ."

Cara nudged Ian with her shoulder so hard she pushed him off balance. "We don't need the travelogue. Go ahead, Ian, say it."

Ian flushed. "My second-in-command likes to take matters into her own hands. She countermanded my order and contacted Ham, Nellie, and Jonah on the emergency system. Nellie is standing by in New York."

"Good thing I sent the signal, too!" Cara exclaimed. "You were attacked, and then thrown out of the mansion!"

"What?" Amy and Dan asked together.

"Literally." Ian winced at the memory. "Bruised my coccyx."

"Your what?" Dan asked.

Hamilton pointed to Ian's butt.

"Ohhh, I get it," Dan said. "They bruised your *brain*?"

"Good one!" Hamilton guffawed, and gave Dan a high five.

"Can we get back to the subject?" Amy asked. She gave Dan the look he called the "sister stink eye," meaning *be quiet or else.*

"Ian!" Cara said. "Say it."

"Ah." A great struggle seemed to take place on Ian's face. "I need your help," he finally blurted.

"Dude, we're retired," Dan said. "Didn't anyone tell you?"

"We know," Hamilton said. "That's why it's a complete bummer that we had to come and find you."

"Don't get me wrong," Dan said. "You're my posse. Happy to see you. Looking good. Et cetera. But you promised us no family business. We are officially Cahill-free. Remember? You took an oath."

"We didn't take an oath," Ian objected.

"You took a *silent* oath," Dan said.

"That's ridiculous," Ian said. "There's no such thing as a *silent* oath. We're oath-less!"

"Will you two knock it off?" Amy said impatiently. She stared Dan down once again.

Sister stink eye to the max!

Ian gestured to the helicopter. "We rented this to take us to Jonah's plane at the Geneva airport. We're just asking for ten minutes of your time. We're on the clock, and we have to decide our next step."

Dan stifled another objection. Of course he had to listen. He got that. These were his best friends. His family. He wouldn't turn his back on them.

And they'd shown up in a very cool helicopter. That was a bonus.

If only he didn't have the feeling that if he climbed aboard, he'd be climbing into a big Cahill mess.

"Where are you going?" Amy asked.

"That's the problem," Cara said. "We don't know yet."

"What about Jake and Atticus?" Amy asked, referring to her boyfriend and his brother. Atticus was Dan's best friend, and the pair had fought hard alongside the Cahills. They'd kept up with them on video conference, and they were as close as ever. "Are you going to contact them, too?"

"The Outcast said no outsiders," Cara said.

The Outcast? It's never good when evil dudes have a nickname.

Dan's feet felt like lead as he climbed aboard the copter. He had to admit, though, that it was one sweet ride. Cream-colored cushy leather seats. A mini-fridge with snacks. A flat-screen TV. It was like a fancy hotel suite with rotors attached.

Dan sat gingerly on the leather seat and listened as Ian filled them in. With a glance at his sister, he could feel Amy's laser-brain honing in on the details, but he kept losing track. It was all so awful. What kind of a slimeball would restage major disasters? Hold lives in the balance?

"Is there any chance this guy is just faking all this?" Dan asked. "Because this just sounds like he's trying to scare us so he can get control."

"He already *has* control," Ian pointed out. "And he's living in Grace's mansion."

"Wait a second," Dan said. "What about Saladin?"

"Saladin, too," Hamilton said. "I hope they feed him red snapper."

"He has my *cat*?"

"So if we don't prevent these disasters, innocent people will be killed," Amy said. "Can we watch the video?"

Dan shot a glance at his sister. Amy just used the word *we*. She'd already made up her mind.

Cara handed over her tablet. Amy and Dan watched it play through. Dan felt a chill run through him from just the sight of the guy.

"Recognize him?" Ian asked, pointing to the Outcast.

Amy and Dan shook their heads.

"How about this guy?" Ian pointed to the man they hadn't been able to ID. "Notice how he's keeping his face averted? He knew where the cameras are."

"I don't recognize him," Amy said.

"The first step is to find out who the Outcast is. He knew Grace. That's clear. Did you notice the way he talked about her? So he's a figure from her past. Remember when he quoted her?"

Dan recited the words. " 'If your best instincts are your worst enemies, take your hands off the controls. Find someone else to fly the plane.' "

"I never heard her say that," Amy said. "Maybe it's in some Cahill archive. An official letter, or memo, or speech . . . maybe we could track him that way."

"I can't get into the archive," Cara said. "I've managed to get our personal phones and tablets hooked up and secure, but we can't tap into the Cahill network. It's like flying blind."

"Keep trying," Amy said. "If anyone can do it, you can. Considering the fact that people don't seem to know him, but he knew Grace, it could be from pretty long ago. Has anyone talked to Uncle Fiske?"

"He's in Mexico for three months," Ian said. "I didn't want to disturb him."

"Nellie should go talk to him. In person."

Ian frowned, and Dan realized that Amy was already snapping orders, even though she wasn't the head of the family anymore. Casually, he nudged her with his foot.

"I mean, if you think that's a good idea, Ian," she added.

"Certainly," Ian said in a chilly tone.

"Sorry, Ian," Amy said. "It's hard to get out of the habit of being the head of the family."

"Indubitably," Ian said.

Jonah held up a hand. "Don't go all Brit-fuff-fuff on us, Kabra. You're the family leader, no question, but we're here looking for Amy's expertise, am I right?"

Ian drew himself up. "I have no idea what you mean. I've never been Brit-fuff-fuff in my life. Whatever that means."

"It means all superior and puffed up," Ham explained.

"Well, that's certainly not me," Ian said. He adjusted the cuffs of his blazer.

Cara laughed. "Sometimes, you're just adorable," she said to Ian. "And sometimes you're just insufferable. You're going all Brit-fuff-fuff right now!"

Silence greeted that remark. No one else had ever connected the word *adorable* with Ian.

"Here's the deal," Jonah said. "We've got ourselves a huge problem. This guy is going to seriously hurt and kill people. Under the Cahill *name*, yo. And we've got less than five days to solve the riddle and stop him. We're already smack in the middle of day one."

"The riddle," Amy said. "Let's hear it again." She cued it up and pressed PLAY.

Your first disaster took place at sea
It was sad—rich and poor died in agony
Broke all records for calamity
For those still clad in pajamity
A collision caused the terrible losses
In the Maritimes you'll find the crosses
On Mont Blanc rest the ones to blame
Oh, to maim, blind, and kill, and have no shame!
It will happen again if you can't stop it
At least the Cahill fam will profit!

"At first we thought it was easy," Ian said.

Dan nodded. "Hello, iceberg, meet *Titanic*!"

"Probably the most famous maritime disaster in history," Amy agreed.

"Loved that movie," Ham said. "Cried like a two-year-old."

"But the *Titanic* didn't blind anyone," Ian said. "That's the thing that stands out. Or maim them. People either drowned or were saved."

"The Maritimes are in Canada," Amy said. "Maybe that's what he's referring to."

"And then there's the Mont Blanc reference," Ian said. "It didn't make sense."

"That's weird, because it's in the Alps, not Canada," Dan said. "As a matter of fact," he added, pointing to the massive mountain framed in the copter window, "it's right *there*."

Amy leaned forward. "Let's plug all the elements that don't make sense into a search engine chain. Canada, Mont Blanc, collision, blindness."

Cara's fingers flew. She raised her head, a look of astonishment on her face. "Wow. This has got to be it. It happened in Halifax, Nova Scotia, in 1917. One of the greatest disasters at sea ever. A French freighter, the *Mont-Blanc*, collided with another ship in the harbor. A fire detonated the cargo of the freighter, which was carrying hundreds of tons of TNT, plus other explosive materials."

"That was during World War I, right?" Amy asked.

Cara nodded as she scrolled through the material. "The ship was heading to the front, so it was packed with explosives for weapons. It was massive. The largest man-made blast before the atomic bomb. It killed almost two thousand people, maiming and *blinding* thousands more, because it blew out almost every window and turned the glass into flying missiles. It happened at 8:45 in the morning."

"While people were having breakfast," Amy said. "Some in their pajamas."

"So this nutcase is going to *re-create* that?" Ham asked. "Blow up a city?"

They sat in silence for a moment.

Jonah got up. "I'll tell my pilot to file a flight plan."

Ian looked at Amy and Dan. "So. Are you in?"

Amy glanced at Dan. He knew she wouldn't answer without checking in with him.

He was the reason they'd gone on this long, aimless journey. What they hadn't been able to admit to each other in the past few months was that maybe they'd grown just the tiniest bit bored. Maybe his life had changed so much that he couldn't go back to being happy just hanging out. So he'd pushed them. From surfing to paragliding. From rock climbing to bungee jumping. From parachuting to wingsuit BASE jumping.

Because after what they'd been through, just being normal wasn't enough.

That didn't mean he wanted to jump right back into this. If he ever wrote a book about his family, the title would probably be *Those Cahills!: Tales of Mayhem, Backstabbing, and Crazy People Who Think They Deserve to Rule the World.*

But no way would he walk away from friends in trouble.

Simple as that.

He didn't have to say a word. Amy recognized his decision. She gave him the tiniest of nods. They were in.

"This guy took over our family," Amy said quietly. "We're going to get it back."

"Plus, he stole my cat," Dan said. "Try and stop me."

Amy stood up. "We'll have to go get our bags," she said.

Ian smiled. "No need. We broke into your hotel room and packed your stuff."

Hamilton slung his muscled arms over Amy's and Dan's shoulders. "Welcome home."

CHAPTER 10

Attleboro, Massachusetts

Nature was cruel. No question about it. Earthquakes, floods, tsunamis . . . natural disasters were all ruthlessly efficient when it came to population reduction.

But when it came to devastation, the Outcast would bet on human stupidity, every time.

He swiped through the images on his screen. He had one last disaster to pick, and it was important not only that the death toll be high, but that it would be symbolic of his eventual victory. Not that the children would necessarily understand this. It would be a small, private pleasure to be savored after he won.

He was close to deciding. The disasters would escalate. Until the last great, impossible task.

He would restore honor to the Cahill family. Glory to the Ekat branch. At last the Ekats would be where they belonged: in the very seat of power. He would use the Tomas, the Lucians, the Janus, but they would just be tools in his hands. Best of all, at the end of a long life, he would live out the rest of his days holding ulti-mate power.

You used to tell me that I wasn't ruthless enough, Grace. Remember?

So I proved that I was.

I had to wait until you were dead to prove it again.

The Outcast turned off the screen. He sat and surveyed Grace's library. It appeared that the grand-children had restored it with a meticulous attention to what it had been. There were changes in the man-sion of which he did not approve—he would rip out that climbing wall, for starters, and the zip line from the attic to the tree house was ridiculous—but the library was as he remembered it, the deep window seats, the wall-to-wall bookcases, the brass telescope, the rich emerald-colored tiles around the fireplace.

All of it belonged to him now.

The Outcast strolled to the telescope and trained it on the drive. His team was just climbing out of a black SUV. He studied them carefully. He had planned this coup for years, and chosen his five conspirators with great precision—grooming them, promising them, flattering them. And noting their weaknesses.

They did not speak as they walked to the front steps. They each kept a few feet of distance between themselves and the rest. Magnus was first, of course, striding toward the front door, his long black coat flapping behind him.

They were suspicious of each other. Most likely despised each other. What difference did it make? They probably despised him, too.

He knew some of them were annoyed that they were not invited to stay at the mansion. Goodness knows it was big enough.

But it was his at last. And he would not share it.

He had rented several apartments for them in Boston instead. Anonymous places, luxurious corporate rentals. Patricia Oh, of course, had demanded a four-star hotel instead.

She was a bore. But useful.

He had known her as a young girl, beautiful and delicate and lethal. Now she was old and brittle. Her hair was unnaturally dark, and there were feathered lines around her thin mouth. Her trademark rubies flashed on her fingers in long columns that led to the knuckle. He knew from experience how those stones could tear your skin with one hard slap.

She was here to avenge Alistair, her cousin. She believed that he'd been duped by Amy and Dan, had turned soft, had betrayed the Ekats.

The Outcast's mouth twisted. What did she know of betrayal? What did anyone know?

The greatest betrayal demands the greatest revenge.

He tilted the telescope back into place as he heard them enter the house. Their footsteps echoed as they traversed the great hall and headed for him.

Patricia entered first, flinging her coat on the wing

chair. He had never seen her in a good mood. "I need strong coffee."

"Good day to you, too," the Outcast said. "Berman has set up coffee and tea on the side table. There's cream and sugar as well."

"I don't take cream. It confuses things." Patricia reached up and patted her elaborate hairdo. Her black hair was piled on top of her head and was anchored there by a large wooden ornament that sat on her head like a crown.

"I don't see why we have to meet in person," Toby Griffon said, adjusting his black-framed glasses. The only reason the Outcast had allowed him into the conspiracy was because he needed a powerful Janus. Toby was a world-famous architect known for exacting demands and tyrannical tirades. But as far as the Outcast was concerned, Janus were undependable. Creative geniuses, sure, but that same originality meant they walked their own path. It didn't matter. Toby was here just to keep the Janus in line.

Magnus remained standing. "I think I can deliver all the Tomas leaders," he said.

"The Ekats are in line," Patricia said. "A few holdouts. The Mourads could turn into a problem."

"Nothing that can't be fixed." The Outcast waved his hand.

"The Lucians are more difficult." Melinda Toth took off her kid gloves, finger by finger. Like all Lucians, she had a sense of drama. She was painfully thin, with a large head that descended into a pointed chin. "Naturally. We are leaders, after all, and so we don't like it when someone else is in charge." She slapped her gloves down on the table. "I can't guarantee I can deliver a unified branch."

"Just get enough support and don't bore me with your difficulties," the Outcast snapped.

"There's a lot of talk about you tossing out Ian Kabra," Melinda said, narrowing her catlike eyes. "Some are saying it was too extreme."

"Mercy is a swift sword," Alek Spasky said. He sat on the floor with his legs crossed in a yoga pose. He was dressed in a pair of loose pants and a tunic. He smiled at the group.

Funny thing about that smile. His eyes never warmed. Those cold, dark eyes. The same chilling gaze his sister had.

Who knew that Irina Spasky had a brother?

The Outcast did. He'd scoured the world, and finally located him in a Zen retreat in California.

Even the monks had looked relieved to see him go.

"And this plan to re-create disasters? It seems extreme," Toby said. "Excess pressure can bring down even the mightiest of structures."

"Did the Buddha say that?" Alek asked.

"No, I did."

"Very deep," Alek said, but his mouth twisted in another of those chilling smiles. Toby flushed as he felt the sting of the sarcasm.

"Toby does have a point," Patricia said. "I can't control my branch if there is too much dissent. We've always operated by stealth. This could be too public."

It was a struggle to keep the smile on his face. *Traitor!* He wanted to scream at Patricia. He had recruited her, groomed her, helped her gain her power. Now she was challenging him? He was certainly rethinking helping make her branch leader.

Alek stood and walked to the silver pots of coffee and hot water. He took a tea bag from his pocket and placed it in a cup, then poured steaming water over it. The Outcast noted the missing tip of his pinkie finger. He must have gotten a bit too close to a sharp blade. "If you two aren't prepared to risk, what are you doing here?" Alek asked in a mild tone. "You approved the plan. If you can't summon up the nerve to follow through . . ."

"Now, hold on a second," Toby said. "I didn't say—"

Patricia's voice was like a cracking whip. "Are you calling me a *coward*, you Russian airhead?" She turned to the Outcast. "I won't be insulted! I told you not to bring him in! He's unstable; everyone knows that!"

The Outcast said nothing. It was better to let them fight it out. See who won. It would be instructive.

"Go back to your mountaintop!" Patricia sneered at Alek. "We don't need you!"

Alek put down his teacup. His fingers moved faster than the Outcast could track. From within his bell-like sleeve he withdrew a steel rod. He twirled it on a finger, so fast it was a blur. The rod flew from his fingers and, spinning and glinting, sped across the room and speared Patricia's hair ornament, lifting it off her head and then pinning it to the wall behind her.

Patricia's hair slipped to one side, and the Outcast realized it was a wig. Toby burst out laughing.

Patricia reached up and readjusted the wig, never taking her eyes off Alek. "You are *despicable*," she hissed.

"I don't like it when people insult me," Alek said, turning and sipping his tea. "Don't do it again."

The Outcast smiled. It had been worth it to track down Alek.

He turned to the others. "The game has begun. The children will be looking into my background. That will be a bore, but it must be handled. There could be some remaining tracks to cover."

"I doubt that," Patricia said huffily. "I was meticulous. Unlike others, I know what I'm doing." She shot Alek Spasky a venomous look.

The Outcast said nothing. He watched as Alek sipped his tea. Dear, ruthless Alek. He would come in handy very soon.

CHAPTER 11

Halifax, Nova Scotia

The late winter wind sliced through Ian as they walked the streets of Halifax toward the harbor. It had snowed the night before, a dusting that still clung to the tree branches and rooftops of the stone and brick buildings of downtown Halifax. Sunlight sent sparkles into Ian's vision. People strolled by wrapped in colorful scarves, smiling at the blue sky and twinkling snow.

Canadians, Ian thought darkly. *Why are they always so happy?*

Even though he was hunched against the chill, Ian's brain was working feverishly. He'd caught up on sleep on the plane from Geneva, but he hadn't had time to develop a plan. Just a direction. He had to come up with something before they hit the harbor. They were already in the morning of the second day, and he could feel the clock ticking.

The ships coming into port were posted online, but the information was sparse. They needed detailed information about cargo, and the only place to get that would be the Port Authority office.

He glanced over at Amy, who was chatting quietly with Hamilton. Had she thought of a plan, but just didn't want to share it until he came up with something? He'd already asked for her help. He didn't want to have to do it again. It would be nice if she would just *volunteer* something.

Ian massaged his temples as if he could squeeze some ideas out of them. His strategic brilliance was his strength, his mojo, as Jonah would say. Somehow his brain didn't seem to be functioning. Instead a movie was playing in his head, a constant loop of the same scenes: His pants falling down. The Outcast appearing on the screen. Being tossed out of the mansion like a bag of garbage.

Cara drifted back toward him, matching her stride to his. "You've been quiet."

"Thinking about failure," Ian said. "It's a new sensation."

"Anyone who risks big, fails big."

"Did you get that from a fortune cookie?" Ian asked bitterly.

"No, I got 'Beware Brit-fuff-fuffs who enjoy feeling sorry for themselves.'"

"Thanks a lot!" Ian said, stung. "The next time I need help, I know where not to go."

Cara sighed. "Why do you have to be such a jerk?"

"I can't help my upbringing," he muttered. "Kabras were raised to be awful."

"So were Pierces. That's why you and I understand each other. We have to fight our genes."

"This is supremely unhelpful."

"Look, I'm just saying, if you're the leader of the Cahills, things are going to go wrong. Like, all the time."

"But did it have to happen while I was standing in my underwear?"

"Okay, that was unfortunate, but—"

"I was humiliated!"

Cara flashed the one dimple that under normal circumstances could disarm him completely. "At least you have nice legs."

"They threw me out! Magnus called me a crybaby!"

"He was trying to get to you! To get inside your head! And have you noticed? It worked!"

Ian said nothing. Better to be silent when you're cornered.

"Do you want my advice?" Cara asked.

"No." Ian stomped on, thrusting his hands in his pockets. If he went to Cara for advice, she'd have the upper hand. Then she'd never think of him as boy-friend material. That's what his father always said. *When it comes to women, Ian, I'll give you this piece of advice: Maintain your superiority at all times.*

Ian paused. Was he really willing to take advice from his father?

He cleared his throat. "Well. If you insist."

"Stop worrying about your stupid dignity and start worrying about the innocent people who just might die because some crazy old guy is making a power grab. You're feeling sorry for yourself, and we don't have time for that. So get over yourself, Kabra."

"Just when I thought I'd get some sympathy!"

"If you want a pep talk, find a different girl. Ian, you've got to stop focusing on yourself and focus on other people. You'd be a lot happier. And a better leader."

She yanked him to a stop. Ian almost slipped on the ice, but she caught him.

"Must you always knock me about?" he complained.

"Yes! Until you listen to me! Really listen!"

Ian faced her. A sudden burst of wind sent the snow flying, a shower of diamonds that drifted into Cara's hair.

"You think I'm an egotistical fool, don't you," he said.

"Well, sure. Everyone does. Because you *are*." One side of her mouth quirked upward in the lopsided smile that always did something squishy to Ian's knees. "But not all the time." She nudged him again, but less fiercely. "There's hope for you yet."

Ian felt his heart swell. His charm was working after all. He still had it. She was softening. He could see it. In the middle of all this trouble and darkness, this would be his light. Cara.

"I don't care what everybody thinks," he said, and was about to add, *I care what you think, very much*, but Cara scowled.

"You should care what they think," she said, gesturing toward the group. "Because they'd go to the wall for you. Until you realize that, no matter how well you do, you'll still be a loser."

With that, Cara turned and marched down the street toward the group, not caring if he followed.

Crikey. That didn't go so well.

She'll come around. They always do. Because you're a Kabra.

Ian pressed his fist to his forehead. This time, he tried to pummel out the memory of Vikram Kabra. *Get out of my head, Father! I don't need your advice!*

He hurried to catch up without looking as though he was hurrying.

"What's our cover story?" Dan asked. "Why would a bunch of kids need shipping records?"

"There isn't a reason," Ian said. This part he'd already figured out. "We have to get Cara into an interior office so she can invade their computer. Do you think you'll be able to access the shipping details?" he asked her.

"Child's play," she said.

"What we need is a distraction," Ian said. "Then add confusion."

Ian nearly collided with a little girl who darted out of a toy store. Her mother ran after her with an apologetic smile. Ian scowled. The little girl wore a blue wool hat pulled down to her eyebrows and carried a big yellow balloon. "Today's my birthday!" she called to Ian.

For a second he was merely irritated. Why did little kids assume that other people wanted to hear their boring trivialities? And no doubt that balloon would just get in the way of pedestrians. Right now it was bobbing in Cara's face, and he couldn't believe how cheerfully she batted it away.

Then he had an idea.

"Happy birthday!" he said to the little girl in his warmest tone. Cara smiled at him. Ian had forgotten how girls thought it was cute when guys were nice to kids. Something to remember for later. He'd rent a whole kindergarten class if it meant Cara would smile at him again.

Maybe that was what he needed to do, plot the conquest of Cara's heart like a Lucian.

But first, it was time to unfurl his brilliant plan.

CHAPTER 12

San Miguel de Allende, Mexico

Nellie and Sammy Mourad stood on the edge of the town square as a large mariachi band played a lively Mexican folk tune. The sound of guitars, violins, and trumpets soared through the mountain air. In the center of the square, dancers swirled in bright yellow skirts. Spectators swayed and sang, applauding the dancers in bursts of joy.

Normally, Nellie would be all over this kind of festivity. She'd be searching out the perfect empanada, chatting with a local, buying an ice cream from a vendor, sipping a tamarind soda. Gazing into the soulful eyes of her gorgeous boyfriend. But now she just shifted impatiently as she searched the crowd. They had stopped at Fiske's house, but the housekeeper had only told them that he was at the festival at the Jardín, which was what everyone called the central square of the town. It seemed impossible to locate him in this crush.

"Let's keep moving," Nellie said to Sammy. When she turned, Sammy was putting away his phone, an anxious look on his face. "What's wrong?"

"I haven't been able to reach my parents," he said. "It's weird that I haven't heard from them. Especially since I told them I was flying to Mexico with you."

"Don't they work all the time? Maybe they're involved in some big experiment." The Mourads were basically geniuses. Sammy's mother was a physicist, and his father was some kind of biochemical trailblazer. Nellie wasn't quite sure. One night in his lab, Sammy had described their studies, and Nellie had fallen asleep in his armchair. She had been too embarrassed to ask him to repeat it.

"Yeah. But they usually check in. Like, right now they should be saying, 'Sammy, you need to study, not run off to Mexico with your girlfriend.'" He smiled, but the worried look didn't leave his face.

Sammy was a graduate student in biochemistry who, until he met her, stayed in his lab to work all hours of the night, studying through holidays and school breaks. Nellie was relieved that his parents seemed to like her, even though she was a Mexican-American part-time college student with platinum streaks in her dark hair, whose aspiration was to run her own pan-global tapas restaurant and who had pulled their son into Cahill family intrigue and, worst of all, was a Red Sox fan.

Suddenly, the crowd began to chant. "El Coyote! El Coyote!"

"Who is that?" Nellie wondered.

The woman standing next to her overheard. "You haven't heard of El Coyote, the great Mexican dancer?"

Just then a blare of trumpets announced the new dancer. A slender figure appeared in the middle of the dancers, as though he'd materialized out of thin air. He was dressed in white pants and a flowing white shirt, and wore a beautifully carved coyote mask over his face.

"El Coyote!" the crowd roared.

Guitars hummed in a menacing tune as he stalked the women, dancing gracefully around them as they pretended to run, leaping and twirling. The trumpets burst forth as the dancer joined the women, pretending to flick his nonexistent skirts at them and copying their movements so expertly that the spectators gave hoots of laughter and applauded again. The dance became a blur of white and yellow as he twirled with the dancers, faster and faster, until they were like flowers in a whirlwind. The crowd around the Jardín roared their approval and more cries of *El Coyote!* thundered through the square.

Nellie shook her head. "He's amazing," she murmured.

"*Un guerrero formidable,*" the woman next to her agreed.

The music ended. The dancers bowed. Laughing, Fiske Cahill removed his coyote mask. His gaze met Nellie's across the square, and his grin slowly faded.

Fiske's rented house was up a twisting cobblestone street from the colonial town. Below them, they could glimpse the pink spire of the church. Sunlight splashed on the charming buildings painted in shades of mango, ocher, and avocado. They sought shelter from the afternoon sun in the courtyard, underneath a spreading laurel tree. Blasts of blooming purple bougainvillea tumbled down the walls of the hacienda. The air was sweet and scented with blossoms.

Trouble seemed very far away.

But trouble darkened Fiske's expression as he watched the video on Nellie's tablet. He tapped on his glass of limeade, his fingers beating a rhythm of anxiety.

"I didn't expect a power grab like this," he said, his gaze far away as he looked over the town. "I thought we'd seen enough calamity for one lifetime. What do we know about this Outcast?"

"We know he's a Cahill, but we can't find out any information on his background," Nellie said. "He's been recruiting for a while, we think."

"I know Magnus," Fiske said. "He was always power hungry. And Patricia is just like her great-uncle."

"What about him?" Nellie asked, zooming in to the man they couldn't identify. "We don't have a clear shot of his face."

Fiske tilted the tablet toward himself. He zoomed in to the man's hand. "Bad news. See that missing finger joint on his pinkie? That's Irina Spasky's brother, Aleksander. Irina was a cupcake compared to him."

"I didn't know she even had a brother," Nellie said.

"He was never an active Lucian. All photos of him mysteriously vanished shortly after his disappearance." Fiske clasped his hands together and bent forward, his face creased in anxiety. "He was an assassin for the KGB."

Nellie felt a chill move through her, despite the sun on her shoulders. "What about the Outcast? Amy thought that since we can't access the digital archives, you might have some idea of who he could be. We know when you were younger, you left the operation of the family to Grace, but we figure this guy is in his eighties, and you might have met him long ago."

"He doesn't look familiar," Fiske said. "He looks as though he's had surgery, though."

"Definitely," Nellie agreed. "What about when he quotes Grace—*If your best instincts are your worst enemies, take your hands off the controls. Find someone else to fly the plane.* Amy thinks it might be significant. Does that sound familiar?"

Fiske shook his head. "No."

Nellie knew Fiske well enough to know that something was troubling him, something more than receiving the news of the takeover. All she had to do was wait.

"It's the name," Fiske said. "Outcast. The name . . . It has a history." Fiske hesitated. "Grace was my sister and I loved her, but she could be . . . ruthless. If she felt someone was undermining the family or putting it at risk, she gave them that label. They were cast out from the family. No contact, no resources. Anyone caught helping them was punished." Fiske hesitated, a pained expression suddenly constricting his features. "They had to leave their immediate family. A complete break with parents, husbands, wives . . . even children. There weren't many Outcasts, but for those it happened to, it was devastating."

Nellie felt as though the world had tilted. She shook her head, unwilling to believe the picture Fiske had just painted. "That doesn't sound like the Grace Amy and Dan talk about," she said. "She sounds . . . cruel."

"There were many sides to Grace," Fiske said. He stirred restlessly. "I always thought it was better not to ask too many questions."

"Do you know who the Outcasts were?" Sammy asked.

"I only knew one."

Nellie leaned forward. "Great! Who?"

Fiske poured himself more limeade. "Me."

"You? But . . ."

"It was my official designation. When I told Grace I wanted nothing to do with the family anymore — after we stayed up all night arguing — she finally conceded. But she wouldn't just let me go. She had to protect me. So she suggested that she make me an Outcast, and I agreed."

"But other Cahills probably assumed that you'd done something terrible," Nellie said.

"That was the price I paid for freedom," Fiske said. "I was glad to pay it. Others were not. If they fought her, they had to suffer retribution."

Slowly, Nellie sank back in her chair. This was a new portrait of Grace. She couldn't reconcile it with the woman who gave so much love to Amy and Dan, who was still a source of guidance in their lives.

"Grace was my sister and I loved her," Fiske said. "But I refuse to idealize her. She felt she had the fate of the world on her shoulders. She knew the serum could be devastating if it got out. I am sure there are things she did that she regretted." Fiske took a gulp of his drink. "She didn't ask my advice. She didn't ask anybody. And she didn't let anyone or anything interfere with what she thought was right."

"What *she* thought was right," Nellie said.

Fiske gave a small, sad smile. "In those days, I didn't approve of some of her methods. Today, when I see what's happened to us since the thirty-nine clues were found . . . today I have more understanding of what she feared."

"So in order to find the Outcast, we need deep background," Sammy said. "Until Cara can hack back into the system, we have nowhere to go."

Fiske nodded. "What you need is someone who was around then, someone with a talent for ferreting out feuds and secrets and who is malicious enough to remember all the details. In other words, the worst person I know."

Nellie almost choked on her limeade. "No. Don't tell me. I can't."

Sammy stirred in alarm. "Who? Another assassin?"

"Worse," Nellie whispered. "Aunt Beatrice."

CHAPTER 13

Halifax, Nova Scotia

Dan held a huge bouquet of balloons. Amy had two enormous boxes of candy. They stood outside the door of the Port Authority.

"Ready?" Ian asked. "Go."

They pushed through the door, crowding in with the balloons. A woman at a reception desk looked up, smiling but confused.

Outside the picture window, ten stories down, massive freighters moved in and out of the harbor and docked at the piers. Tall orange cranes extended hundreds of feet in the air. In the distance, lacy curls of foam danced on the water as a blue-and-white ferry chugged across the harbor.

"Can I help you?"

"We came to see our parents off at the ship!" Amy said. "They're sailing today, and we need to catch them. It's a second honeymoon! We're not too late, are we?"

"The cruise ships are farther down the pier," the woman said. "You're in the harbormaster's office."

"Told you!" Amy said to Dan.

Dan spoke to the woman. "Can you hold my balloons while I check my phone? I just want to send a text."

"I hardly think—"

The door opened and Cara hurried in.

"We're here to pick up some bulk cargo? My dad's waiting in the truck outside," Cara said breathlessly. "Can you help us?"

"You're in the wrong place . . . if you'll just wait a moment. We're terribly busy today. Winter storm approaching, and we have to get the ships into port . . ."

Dan let the balloons go. They bounced and twirled, twining around each other, and one bopped the woman in the head. "Whoa, cowboy!" she called good-naturedly. "Can you corral those?"

"Sure," Dan said. He leaped up, trying to grab a fistful of strings. The balloons jiggled and jounced. Dan kept leaping.

"This isn't where you pick up bulk cargo," the woman said to Cara. "It's the next building over."

"Can you show me? I'm directionally challenged!"

The door opened again and Jonah walked in.

Everyone froze.

Cara shrieked, "OMG! Jonah WIZARD!"

Employees suddenly spilled out from inner offices. They crowded around Jonah, thrusting pads at him to autograph. Balloons popped. Amy distributed candy. Someone called, "Hey, Mr. Hannigan, get in here!" and a man in a gray suit and a yellow tie hurried out with a great deal of authority.

He stopped dead when he saw Jonah. "This—this is an honor. I'm your biggest fan. Can I take a selfie of us?"

Cara slipped past the barrier and down the back corridor. Amy positioned herself as lookout.

So far, Ian's plan was working.

"Let's keep it quiet, homies," Jonah said in that confiding tone that always melted resistance. "I'm in town because I just signed for a new movie called *HARBORMASTER!* That's with an exclamation point, bro! It's an action-adventure thriller, and I play a young harbormaster learning the tricks of the trade from the old guy who's retiring. Plus, I have a little sister who needs an operation! Conflict, heartbreak, a terrorist plot to blow up the harbor . . . it's got it all."

"Thrilling!" the woman at the reception desk exclaimed.

"Nobody appreciates how interesting it is at a harbor," a man said. "Right, Mr. Hannigan?"

"The tonnage we've got coming in and out every day, it's a big responsibility," Mr. Hannigan said. "It's got to go like clockwork."

"That's exactly why I'm doing this movie!" Jonah widened his eyes. "You guys are heroes, keeping track of all those boats."

"We call them ships," Mr. Hannigan said.

"You see? There's so much I have to learn!"

Soon everyone competed to fill Jonah in on the workings of the port. Out of the buzz of conversation, Amy only caught snatches. "Container gantries," "straddle carriers," and "transtainers" met with respectful "whoas" from Jonah. Amy felt time ticking by as though it was a physical dance on her nerves. There were only two people left in line to take selfies with Jonah. *Hurry up, Cara!*

She let out a breath of relief when Cara came up behind her. "Got it," she whispered. Amy signaled Jonah.

"This has been supremely enlightening and a huge mondo help," Jonah said. "But I have an interview with *Vanity Fair*, and I've got to roll."

CHAPTER 14

Ignoring the cold wind whipping in from the water, the gang climbed the fence marked NO ADMITTANCE and wove their way through the cranes and trucks and giant containers to the pier. Towering over them was a massive cargo container ship as big as a building.

Amy shivered in the icy wind off the harbor. She had to crane her neck to see the top of the bow of the ship, maybe fifty feet up. The ship was as long as a football field, and she couldn't imagine what incredible feat of engineering kept it upright in the water. If it tipped over, it seemed as though it would smash them into the center of the earth.

They shrank against the tall metal container, keeping close. Around them, men strode by in hard hats, heading to cranes, talking on walkie-talkies, consulting clipboards and tablets. Tall orange cranes bristled in the sky like gigantic, clever insects with enormous claws. Various smaller cranes, forklifts, and cargo gear sat next to row upon row of metal containers as big as railroad cars.

Rows and rows, stacks and stacks, hundreds of containers, stretching from one end of the yard to the other.

"They're filled with machine parts," Cara said, reading from the list.

"Nothing that would blow up," Dan said.

"My good man Hannigan said that the containers are sealed at the port of origin," Jonah said. "They don't get opened until the destination. It's all coded and scanned. The crew usually doesn't know what's in those containers—they could be toys from China or sweaters from Thailand or faucets or pipes. . . . The goal is to unload the ship in twenty-four hours. Just load those babies onto trucks and railroad cars."

"So getting inside them would be a problem," Ian said.

"There's nothing on this list that is potentially explosive," Cara said, frowning at her tablet. "Just tractor parts and lumber and things like that. No fertilizer, even. There's another pier that handles cars, and another with bulk cargo, like wheat and grains and soybeans. In other words, nothing on the list looks dangerous."

"Even if we could get into the containers, we'd never be able to open them all," Hamilton said.

"Plus, there'll be inspectors and foremen all over the place when the joint really gets jumping," Jonah said.

"How do we know that the ship we're looking for will even dock?" Amy asked. "What if it's going to blow up out in the harbor like the one in 1917?"

The questions hung in the salty, cold air. The ship looming over their heads seemed to slam down on them, boxing them in.

Amy glanced at Ian. He was staring at the pier, and she could tell he was shuffling through his options. She knew what her next move would be, and she itched to say something.

"Four days left," Cara said. "Well, three and a half, since it's midafternoon."

"Wait a second," Dan said. "Did you hear what the woman said in the harbormaster's office? There's a storm brewing, and they're trying to get all the ships into port. That means that the timeline could speed up."

"Not good news, dude," Hamilton said.

"We need some reconnaissance work," Ian said. "Talk to the dockworkers. Get a sense of the process of unloading, and how tight the security is and how it works. Let's find out if the storm is changing the schedule. Look, there's a bunch of them sitting over there having lunch." He knotted his cashmere scarf more securely around his neck. "I'll stroll over and see what I can find out."

The rest of them exchanged dubious glances.

"Bro, if you think you can pass for a dockworker, you are insane," Jonah said. "You're wearing cashmere."

"Lucians have marvelous powers of deception," Ian said.

"I can hear you now," Dan said. He mimicked Ian's posh accent. "'Good day, chaps, I merely strolled down here to have a spot of chat.' They'll keelhaul you and feed you to the oysters."

Ian tried to look annoyed, but he shrugged. "I can't help it if I have class and sophistication. What we really need is some brawny fellow who will fit in."

Everyone looked at Hamilton.

"Hey!" Hamilton protested. "I have class, too!"

"We should split up," Ian said. "Hamilton, you pretend to be looking for work. I'll pretend to be a clueless guy looking for a way to ship something or other. Meanwhile, Jonah and Dan can try to get aboard a ship. Jonah, just keep talking about the movie you're going to make. See how far you can get." Ian glanced at Amy and Cara. "As for you two . . ."

"We'd be too conspicuous," Amy said. "There doesn't seem to be a female contingent on the piers. We can walk down to the cruise ship piers. Check them out."

"Exactly what I was thinking. Let's meet back at the motel," Ian said. He checked his watch. "In two hours."

After a half hour at the cruise ship pier, Amy and Cara had to give up. There was only one ship in port. The cruise season didn't start until May. The chilly weather had driven most people indoors, and there was nobody to ask about the cruise ships.

"I have a feeling we're on the wrong track anyway," Amy said. "Maybe the boys will have better luck."

Cara shivered against the cold wind. "What do you say we find some hot chocolate before we head to the pier?"

Amy didn't answer. She stared out at the wind-whipped harbor, thinking hard. "We're making a mistake."

"Sending Ian to talk to dockworkers? Disaster."

"What is he after, anyway?"

"Ian? Most likely a cup of Earl Grey tea about now."

"No," Amy said. She stared out at the harbor as if her enemy would suddenly materialize. "The Outcast."

"What does any evil guy want? Power."

Amy frowned. "So why didn't he just take over and edge us out? Why *test* us?"

"I don't know." Cara cocked her head, looking at Amy. "Do you?"

"He wants to humiliate us," Amy declared. "He wants the entire Cahill network to judge us as incompetent children. The question is, *then what?* The guy has an endgame. I just wish I knew what it was. It would help us fight him. We have to get inside his head."

"The lives that might be lost aren't real to him. People are pawns in a game."

Amy nodded. "Exactly. We saw today that it would be close to impossible to discover all the cargo that comes into this port. We could spend days, weeks trying to investigate. Is that what the Outcast wants?"

"Well, yeah," Cara said. "Isn't that the whole point?"

Amy shook her head. "No. If he makes it impossible, it's not a *contest.* He has to impress the rest of the Cahills with his ingenuity. It's got to beat ours. Can you think of any Cahill who would be impressed with someone who can plant a bomb on a ship? Or trigger some explosive cargo?"

"I see your point," Cara said, a surge of excitement in her voice as she realized where Amy was going. "Child's play for a Cahill. So it would have to be something interesting, some leap of technology or inventiveness. Something to show the family that he's smarter than we are. Right?"

"Exactly. What if there wasn't a bomb? What if the ship itself was a bomb, just like in 1917?"

"But there are no ships carrying weapons coming into port. We already found that out."

"That we know of."

"Smugglers," Cara said. "Weapons trafficking."

Amy nodded. "But that leaves us worse than

nowhere. That means hidden cargo. Secret manifests. How could we possibly find it?"

"Unless we happen to know a major arms trafficker."

"Right. But who would know someone like that?"

Cara's face flushed. "I do."

CHAPTER 15

Sleet tapped against the steamy windows of the coffee shop. Outside looked blurry and unreal. Cara leaned in closer to Amy so that her voice wouldn't carry. "When I was working for Pierce, he asked me to contact this guy Atlas," she said. "I didn't know why at first. I just had to find the guy. It wasn't easy—he had an e-mail address that kept bouncing back. Fake IP addresses, servers . . . I was tracing it all over the place, from China to India to Sri Lanka. Finally I tracked him down. That's when I figured out that Pierce was going for nukes."

"Pretty twisted," Amy said.

"Story of my childhood," Cara said crisply. "Not my point. If I'd known who he was, I never would have found him for Pierce. Do you see what I'm saying? He is a nasty guy. The worst. He doesn't live anywhere. Always on the move. He's not one of those flashy types who has a legitimate business to hide behind. Just shell companies that don't really exist."

"So this guy is really connected to the weapons trade."

"He basically *is* the global weapons trade. If there's a big shipment, he's probably involved. While you were getting the drinks, I put all the ship information through my search engine to see if it came up with a match of any of Atlas's fake companies. No match, but . . . I found out that the captain of a ship coming into port once worked for one of them. He's the captain of the cargo ship *Aurora*."

"Do you think the ship might be smuggling weapons?"

"Don't you?"

"If we can get aboard the *Aurora* . . ." Amy said.

"We might be able to find whatever it is that is going to trigger an explosion. But we need a solid intro to the captain. If we offer Atlas enough money, he might come and meet us. He always meets people face-to-face the first time."

"We'll have to pose as customers to bait the trap," Amy said.

"This could be dangerous," Cara said. "I'm not saying we shouldn't do it. I'm just saying . . . he's a really, really bad guy."

"But we don't have any time to waste," Amy argued. "Why don't you send out an e-mail right now? We can always change our minds."

Cara quickly tapped out a brief e-mail. "I hope we don't have to do this. Maybe the guys will get lucky."

Ian, Ham, Jonah, and Dan walked into the motel looking wet and bedraggled. Ham gave the girls a thumbs-down.

Ian grabbed a towel from the bathroom and wiped the rain off his face. "Dockworkers are an extremely uncooperative bunch," he said.

"I saw Jonah pull out every trick in his celebrity handbook," Dan said. "We still couldn't get aboard that ship."

"I found out from some guys that Dan was right," Hamilton said. "The storm is driving the ships into port ahead of schedule. They're going at top speed. So we might be dealing with one or two days until disaster, not three."

"Cara and I have been talking." Amy quickly filled them in on contacting Atlas.

"Thank you for informing me of this major decision," Ian said in a chilly voice. He wadded up his towel and tossed it on the bed. Amy knew he must be really upset. Ian would never toss a wet towel on a bed. "Don't you think we should have all had a vote in this?"

"It's not a decision," Amy said quickly. "We haven't set up the meeting. We just wanted options."

"Well, this is certainly a dangerous one," Ian said. "Meeting with a weapons trafficker?"

"Do we have a choice?" Dan asked. "Our guy is going to blow up a city. Whatever we're dealing with here, it sure isn't tractor parts."

Ian hesitated. "I realize that we don't have a choice. I just don't like this."

"Who knows if he'll even contact us?" Cara pointed out.

Just then her phone buzzed.

She bit her lip. "He wants to meet," she said.

CHAPTER 16

San Miguel de Allende, Mexico / Boston, Massachusetts

Aunt Beatrice's face loomed on the computer. "I don't have time to talk to you now! I leave for Palm Beach tomorrow!" She walked across the room and disappeared. Her voice came to them faintly. "I have to pack! Now, where are my light cashmeres?"

"You have to stay in front of the computer, Aunt Beatrice!" Nellie yelled.

"How can I do that if I have to pack?"

"We can't hear you if you get out of range! WE JUST NEED A FEW MINUTES! DON'T GO IN THE . . ." Nellie slumped back. "Bedroom," she said in a despairing voice.

"I try to videoconference with her," Fiske said. "Part of my brotherly duties. She hasn't quite gotten the hang of it. It's like she expects me to follow her around. Reminds me of my childhood. In other words, depressing and annoying."

"So what do you do?" Sammy asked.

Fiske shrugged. "Eventually, I just give up."

"We don't have time to go to Boston and see her," Nellie said. "This is impossible."

"Wait, she's coming back!" Sammy exclaimed.

Nellie shot forward. "AUNT BEATRICE! WE'RE STILL HERE!"

"I know you are, Nellie," Aunt Beatrice said. "No need to shout. And why do you call me 'aunt' when I'm not your aunt? You're not even a Cahill, technically. I mean, not by birth." Aunt Beatrice made a face. "I don't approve of this Outcast person taking over the family—because, after all, who are his parents?—but he might have a point about the youth taking over. I admit you had some early successes, but where is the *wisdom*? My potential, for example, has been entirely untapped. It's obvious that I'm temperamentally a Lucian, due to my leadership qualities. Though my first husband always said I must be a Janus because of my creativity. And a Tomas because I always beat him at tennis. Oh, he was a lovely man. Until he divorced me. Then he was evil."

"Aunt Beatrice, if we could just stay on the subject—"

"But I am on the subject. My leadership qualities are why Patricia invited me to Singapore to meet the Outcast a few months ago."

"What?" Nellie exploded.

"Well, she didn't call him that. She just said there was a fascinating man I had to meet who had onderful ideas on how to manage the family. Naturally I said no. I smelled something fishy, and even though there are some sublime Singapore fish dishes, I wasn't about to go."

"That doesn't make any sense," Sammy whispered to Nellie.

"Just roll with it," she murmured, her eyes on the screen.

"Besides, I detest those long flights. My ankles swell—"

"Singapore?" Nellie asked. "What happened?"

"I don't know, do I, because I didn't go," Beatrice snapped. "Keep up, dear. Patricia was very put out. She said this person had big plans, and I'd be sorry. That he could . . . What was the word? *Professionalize* us. Is that even a word?"

"Wait a second," Fiske said. "Are you saying you knew about the takeover?"

"Of course not! Nobody said anything about a takeover, and they completely misjudged me if they thought I would approve. I may not agree with putting this young whippersnapper Kabra in charge, but he was chosen and then approved, and if we start overthrowing things, we'll be no worse than that horrible Rasputin, who shouldn't be a Cahill at all. Talk about outcasts!"

Nellie pressed her fingers against her eyes. "Aunt Beatrice, please. Can we stick to the point? Was the Outcast in Singapore?"

"Yes, I said it three times, didn't I? When Patricia said he'd been an Outcast, I just assumed he was one of the Cahills who Grace had booted out of the family. Some of them were quite charming, you know. Despite their wrongdoings. Take Fiske here—when he isn't glowering at me, he can be quite pleasant."

"I've told you," Fiske said with an edge to his voice, "over and over, Grace made me an Outcast to protect me."

"So you say. I don't ask questions, and I'm not a gossip."

Fiske snorted.

"So you don't know who the Outcast is?" Nellie asked.

"I only know what I told you. I didn't pursue it. To tell you the truth, I never liked Patricia all that much."

"Can we talk about Grace's enemies?"

"That Patricia—all she cares about is money, shopping, and her position. She was furious when her cousin Alistair—what is that expression, went rogue?—and helped Amy and Dan."

"Can we get back to my original question?" Nellie asked.

"No, I haven't found my light cashmeres," Aunt Beatrice said. "And you know perfectly well I can't go to Palm Beach without them."

"Not about sweaters! About Grace! Did she have any enemies?"

Aunt Beatrice laughed. "Are you serious? Enemies?

You might as well have asked if she owned *shoes.* Over the course of years, she managed to infuriate anybody who was anybody in the Cahill family. People would swear they'd never talk to her again! Me included. I could sit here and count them for you, but then I'd never catch my plane!"

"Did you know any of the Outcasts?" Nellie asked.

Aunt Beatrice waved a hand. "Of course. Cousin Delphine, John Beame Cahill, Trudy Macon-Fling, and poor Stephano, my second husband . . . I realize he did embezzle from the Cahill treasury, but you'd think a little forgiveness for her own brother-in-law was in order. But Grace never forgave anybody. Her retribution list was endless." Aunt Beatrice leaned closer. "Don't you know that Grace wasn't a nice person? She was mean and petty!"

"Come on now, Bea," Fiske said. "Grace had her issues, but—"

"Don't talk to me, baby brother," Beatrice snapped. "You were always her favorite, and she could do no wrong in your eyes. And may I remind you that you were floating around the Riviera when Grace was head of the Cahills? How would you know what she did?"

"I knew enough," Fiske said. "She was tough, but honorable. She had high standards—"

"She had *ridiculous* standards! Look what she did to her own husband! You are a fool, Fiske Cahill. You always were about Grace. You are still blind. You refuse to admit what she did." Aunt Beatrice's voice shook with bitterness.

Nellie glanced at Sammy. Suddenly, the tension in the room was thick. Fiske gripped the arms of his chair as though he wanted to launch himself through the computer screen.

"It's time you face up to what she really was. What she was capable of," Beatrice said.

"Beatrice, don't." Fiske's tone rang with steel.

"You want information, don't you? Try this." Beatrice leaned closer to the screen. "Grace made her own husband, Nathaniel Hartford, an Outcast."

"What did he do?" Nellie asked.

"He told her he wanted a divorce. That's all."

"You don't know that!" Fiske cried. "She would never make him an Outcast just because her marriage was over!"

"I know about her *pride*," Beatrice sneered. "And her inability to admit failure! So yes, she made him an Outcast because he rejected her. And not only that—"

"Beatrice, I'm warning you—"

"Warning me? Just like Grace? Your precious Grace? Well, I didn't listen to her, and I'm not listening to you! Grace put out a kill order on her own husband!" Aunt Beatrice's words came out in a rush, and she sat back, satisfied.

"That was just a rumor!" Fiske thundered.

"Fine. Believe what you want." Aunt Beatrice glared at the screen. "He's still dead. He was killed in Moscow. Poisoned!"

"What?" Nellie blurted. "I never heard this! It can't be true. Grace wouldn't put out a kill order on anyone!"

"Don't be naive, child. Of course she would! And did! She was ruthless. She did it, and then she scrubbed the archives. But we all know the truth." She shook her finger at the screen. "You are all so blind! Don't you understand? Grace was evil!"

"That's *enough*, Bea," Fiske said, unfolding from the chair and standing in front of the computer. He pointed his finger at the image of Beatrice on the screen. In his billowing white shirt he looked like an avenging angel. "It's *you* who is full of malice!"

"I do have a sense of loyalty left, no matter what you think, Fiske, and no matter what Grace was. I wouldn't get mixed up with that Outcast. But I'm not going to pretend my sister was an angel. I'm not! And don't point your finger at me!"

Fiske turned away. He was shaking with anger. "This conversation is over."

"I'm sorry, Fiske," Nellie said, glancing from Beatrice's tight face to Fiske's back. "But whatever Grace did or didn't do, the fact remains that one of the Outcasts is out for revenge. There's a pattern here. Ian said Magnus Hansen was involved in the conspiracy. Vikram Kabra. Patricia Oh. They are all people who have been disgraced for some reason or another. Who were forced out of leadership positions. It gives us something to go on."

"And Singapore," Sammy said. "If the Outcast was recruiting from there, someone must know about it. And I know just who to ask. My godparents, the Chens, are prominent Ekats in Singapore. He went to Oxford with my dad."

"No time to waste," Nellie said.

"I'm still here, you know," Aunt Beatrice said. "If you go to Singapore, bring me back some of that divine silk. Pink. I'll give you the address. I have the most talented dressmaker in Palm Beach. . . ."

Fiske strode across the room and switched off the video feed. He crossed to the window and stared out into the courtyard. Nellie studied the stern lines of his face. Anger had changed the set of his mouth. She found to her surprise that he looked much more like the pictures of Grace she'd seen. She'd never thought they looked alike before.

Sammy called softly from across the room, where he was staring at his phone. "We can just catch a connecting flight to Singapore from Mexico City if we leave now."

Nellie nodded at Sammy, then turned back to Fiske. "You said that if any of the Outcasts crossed Grace, they would suffer retribution. You may not believe what Beatrice said, but how far do you think Grace would go? You have to tell me. It's important."

"The past is the past," Fiske said tightly. "Leave it."

"But it's *not* the past!" Nellie argued. "It might be the key to identifying the Outcast!" She put a hand on his arm. "Fiske, tell me. *How far would Grace go?*"

She saw him swallow. His eyes were haunted.

"I don't know," he said.

CHAPTER 17

Halifax, Nova Scotia

At noon, the gang gathered behind a tall stone monument in a square in downtown Halifax. They stared at a white shingled church with a green steeple at the south end of the square.

"It's beautiful," Cara said. "St. Paul's Church. The oldest building in Halifax, built in the seventeen hundreds. It survived the explosion in 1917."

"It even has a ghost," Dan said. "Look at this window!" He held up his phone and showed them a picture of one of the stained glass windows. A profile was clearly shadowed in the pattern of the once-shattered glass.

He read from his phone. " 'In the explosion, the window shattered in the form of the profile of the one-time assistant at the church. He is said to still haunt the aisles.' Boo!"

"We've got enough on our hands without a ghost," Amy said. "We picked it because it's on the tourist track, and we've got exits if we have to get out fast. Cara, if you hang out in City Hall, will you be close enough to hack into Atlas's phone?"

Cara nodded. "Already checked it out. The longer you keep him talking, the more chance I'll have. He'll have firewall after firewall."

Amy walked a few steps closer. She had already studied the church online. It seemed like the perfect place for the meeting. Met all requirements.

She was still nervous.

Ian joined her. "I've gone over it and over it in my head," he said. "We'll be okay."

"Things could go wrong that you don't expect," Amy said.

"I've planned for every eventuality," Ian said. "This is a business meeting. He either agrees to help us or he doesn't."

"True," Amy said. "But this is a guy who's dealt with the baddest people on the planet. He could be unpredictable."

Amy heard the chime of a text and glanced at her phone. A surge of happiness made her face burn. It was from Jake.

Heading off to the farther dig for two weeks. Will be off the grid. Miss u.

Me 2, Amy replied.

```
Thinking about heading back to Harvard
next year. Ready to come home. Atticus
too. Cambridge is close to Attleboro.
Will u be done with your Swift
wanderings by then? Might be nice
to live on the same continent as my
girlfriend.
```

Amy stared down at the text. The prospect of a normal life hummed in her hand. Possibility. Back to Massachusetts, back to Jake. Seeing him, being with him, continuing on this journey of getting to know each other. Was she ready?

Was she *ready*?

She felt giddy just thinking about it.

Across the globe, Jake sat waiting for her answer. She couldn't tell him that the house in Attleboro could be gone forever. She had to see that future, and trust that she could make it true.

```
Sounds perfect. Yes. YES!
```

The answer came back swiftly.

```
I am smiling.
```

Amy pressed *xo* and turned off the phone. She felt her heart lift on the breeze and skid over the rooftops.

She caught Ian looking at her and tried to suppress her smile. "Sorry. It was Jake."

"How do you do that?" Ian asked.

"What?"

"Be *happy* with someone," Ian blurted.

Amy almost laughed, but she saw it was a serious question. "Well, I'm hardly an expert," she said. "The first time I met Jake, I hit him. Hard. Then we didn't want to admit we liked each other. Then we got together. Then we broke up. We got back together. There were whole months that it seemed like all we did was argue."

"That sounds familiar," Ian said.

"And then . . ."

"And then?"

"We decided to trust each other."

Ian looked at her with such an expression of bewilderment on his face that she was tempted to laugh again, but bit her lip instead.

"Lucians don't trust people," he said.

There probably would have been a time when Amy would have nodded and accepted that. All those divisions that kept the Cahill branches apart. Lucians are sly; Ekats can fix anything; Janus are the life of the party; if you want to move a refrigerator, ask a Tomas! But Cahills weren't just about different branches. They were *people*. Individual, quirky people with their own histories and likes and dislikes and their own secret sorrows and their own secret joys.

"Oh, please," Amy said. "That's your father talking. Of course you trust people! You trusted your sister. You trust me, and Dan, and the rest of us. Now you just take one more step. You have to trust the person who can break your heart." She nudged him with her shoulder.

"Why do girls *do* that?" Ian said in exasperation.

"Because boys don't listen hard enough. C'mon, let's get back to the others. We've only got another hour before Atlas shows up. Time to check the perimeter."

They rejoined the others. "So who goes to the meeting?" Dan asked.

Everyone looked at Amy, but she looked at Ian. She felt the need to speak pressing against her throat, but she had to respect Ian's leadership. Still, it was *hard* to have to constantly keep her mouth shut.

"Jonah is too public," Ian said.

"This face is too pretty, yo," Jonah said. "But I'm your backup if something goes south."

"You and Cara," Ian said, nodding. "He answered the e-mail so quickly not because he needs the work. He knows about the Cahills."

"How can you be so sure?" Amy asked.

"Because he's an underground presence, just as we are," Ian said. "He thinks we have unlimited resources and he knows we're powerful. But clearly he does *not* know about the attempted takeover of the family and that we essentially would be without the cash to pay him his fee—if we didn't have Jonah's Hollywood bankroll."

"What's mine is yours, cuz," Jonah said.

"So let's stick to our story. No embellishments."

Amy was glad to see that Ian was back in his usual mode. Giving orders. It was a good sign.

"When you're trying to get something out of someone who is suspicious of you," Ian said, "you have to use the KISS method."

"You have to *kiss* him?" Dan cried. "Gross!"

"Keep It Simple, Stupid," Ian explained. "K-I-S-S. The more details you give, the more holes in the story. We just have to pay him for information. It's all about the money. We'll tell him we have to get on that ship. He doesn't have to know why. If he balks, we intimidate him."

Amy opened her mouth, then snapped it closed. She didn't think intimidation would work with this guy. But she couldn't undermine Ian in front of the others. Besides, he could be right.

Behind her back, she crossed her fingers.

Keep it simple. And hope for luck.

CHAPTER 18

St. Paul's Church, Halifax, Nova Scotia

The man in the black wool cap looked like a tourist. He sat in a back pew, a missal in his hands. He wore a down jacket and jeans. When Amy and Ian slipped in next to him, he didn't turn.

Amy could only see the side of his face. Thin mouth, red beard, thick hands. A gigantic steel watch strapped to one wrist.

Just an ordinary-looking guy.

Then he turned to scope them out, and she felt her stomach drop. In that brief instant of meeting his eyes, she knew she'd just looked into a person without a soul.

A person who trafficked in nuclear weapons. Who tested and sold those weapons to rogue nations, dictators, terrorists. Just for money.

Amy felt fear drop over her like a suffocating hood. She had to force herself to breathe, in and out, trying to get a sense of calm in a suddenly rocking world. She felt dizzy. She reminded herself that Hamilton and Dan were nearby, pretending to be tourists with brochures in their hands, checking out the stained glass windows.

She regretted choosing this meeting place. They had been looking for a central location. Quiet but not too quiet. Maybe a few tourists for cover. More than one exit and streets to get lost in if things went wrong. It fit the bill.

She didn't realize how terrible this would feel. She'd brought evil into this beautiful, sacred space.

Keep your head in the game, Amy.

Ian showed no outward sign of nerves. He did the thing that Ian did when he was nervous. He lifted his chin and looked superior.

"Did nursery school let out?" The man's voice was low and flat. "I didn't realize I was dealing with a couple of kids."

"Cahills," Ian said. "And I'm the head of the Cahill family. I think you're familiar with our resources."

Amy admired Ian's cool. They were in over their heads. Surely he knew it, too.

"I trust you checked out the account numbers we provided," Ian said.

"Wouldn't be sitting here if I hadn't. I only deal with legitimate clients. Sure, you have the resources, but I'm not in this game to play with children." He made a restless move, as though he was about to rise.

"We have plenty of information on your activities," Ian said. "We know exactly what you do. We know that you run nukes all over the world."

No, Amy thought. *No, Ian! Too soon!* Under the cover of the pew, she pressed her foot against Ian's. Telling him to stop. They wouldn't get anywhere threatening Atlas.

Ian pressed back, as if to tell her to chill.

"We know that you're the one to ask about trafficking and weapons," Ian said. "We'll pay you for information."

"You mean sell out my clients?"

"Not necessarily," Ian said. "We are interested in just one ship. The *Aurora*."

"I've got many ships around the world. Hard to remember each one."

"Try."

"I might be familiar with it."

"It's registered as carrying refrigerators to Suriname. I'm sure the authorities here would be interested to know what's actually in the cargo hold."

Don't threaten him, Ian!

"However, we just want to get aboard."

"You want to get aboard?" Atlas raked Ian with a glance.

Ian gave a shrug. "We're not interfering with anyone's profit. We just want to have a look at the ship."

"Why?"

Keep it simple, Ian!

"That's not your concern. All we need is for you to smooth the way with your captain."

"You do know, don't you, that crossing me is something you really don't want to do?"

The voice was low and even, almost lazy. But Amy didn't have to work to hear the menace in it.

"We have no intention of crossing you," Ian said.

Atlas held Ian's gaze for so long that Amy almost screamed *STOP!*

Then he smiled without humor. He slapped both hands on his thighs and stood up. "Then let's go."

"Now?"

"Now or never. Bad weather coming. The *Aurora* is at maximum speed, heading into port. She's three days ahead of schedule. We can head out and meet her. I have a boat."

"You mean you'll pilot the two of us out there?"

"The four of you." Atlas pointed to Dan and Hamilton with his chin. "Tell your friends we're leaving."

CHAPTER 19

Halifax Harbor, Nova Scotia

Dan zipped his jacket up to his neck. He was only wearing a hoodie underneath, and the wind off the water was like a knife. The temperature seemed to be dropping by the minute, and the sky was lowering. The harbor was flecked with white. Boats chugged in and out. A cool mist beaded up on his eyelashes.

Dan could feel the presence of Jonah and Cara following them, but what could they do without a boat? In a silent exchange of looks, Amy, Ian, Hamilton, and Dan had agreed to go along with Atlas. They could be walking into danger, but they had to get on that ship. Dan couldn't imagine another disaster leveling this beautiful city. The number of casualties could be greater even than the blast in 1917. He thought of that little girl with the balloon, skipping away down the street, holding her mother's hand. Something tightened inside him. He wasn't going to back down now.

Atlas led them down a dock to a cabin cruiser. He jumped on board and crossed to the pilot's chair. He started the engine without waiting to see if they followed.

"I don't like this," Ian said softly.

"It feels iffy," Ham agreed.

"You think?" Dan muttered. "We're relying on a guy we can't trust and searching a ship full of weapons to see how and when they're going to blow up. What could possibly go wrong?"

"We've all got tracking devices on our phones," Amy said. "The others will know where we are, at least. And we don't have a better plan."

"Ready to cast off?" Atlas yelled over the sound of the engine. "Or have you changed your minds?"

Dan hated the sneer on his face. He was the first one to leap onto the deck. Ian and Amy followed.

Ham cast off and jumped aboard.

Atlas held out a black cap. "Phones."

They looked at each other, then back at him, unwilling to hand them over.

He shook the cap impatiently. "Phones or no deal. Just in case you're not who you say you are. I don't want police on my tail. You'll get them back when we return."

Reluctantly, they tossed their phones in the cap. He reached in and switched them all off. "Okay. Anchors aweigh."

He tossed the cap on the pilot seat. Standing, he motored out through the moorings, handling the boat with ease. Dan watched the shoreline recede. He noticed that most of the boats, if not all, were heading into the harbor, not out. The sky was dark gray, and even darker clouds were rolling in.

Out here, the mist felt more like rain. He pulled up the hood of his sweatshirt.

They passed under a bridge and hit the break-water. Atlas opened up the throttle. Dan felt his trepidation rise. The boat bumped on the choppy water. Spray mingled with rain, hitting his face like cold needles. He hunched his shoulders, turning away from the wind.

"You okay?" Amy drifted closer.

He nodded. He was cold and wet, and his skin crawled when he thought about what would happen next. But wherever "okay" was on the spectrum, he was there. Because they had to do this.

"We're going to have to cut across the shipping lanes," Atlas shouted over the wind.

Dan nodded, setting his teeth against their impulse to chatter. He saw an enormous tanker in the distance. Atlas seemed to be heading right for it. It grew larger and larger, a floating island, a hundred feet tall. The noise of the engines was louder than the wind.

Was this guy crazy? The tanker was going to smash them into smithereens!

Laughing, Atlas cut the wheel, and they turned sharply to starboard. The wake of the tanker made them roll crazily. Dan saw the sea rush up toward his face, and he had to grab the railing to keep his balance.

"Just making sure you're awake," Atlas shouted.

Ian's face looked green. He hung on to the railing, staring back at the land.

In the distance through wispy fog, another huge container ship was heading into the harbor. This one was even bigger than the tanker, as wide and twice as long as a football field.

Ian pointed.

"Is that it, Mr. Atlas?"

"Looks like it. Let's get a little closer!"

"Great," Dan muttered under his breath.

It was getting darker. It wasn't even five P.M., and dusk was settling in.

"You'd better switch on the running lights!" Dan yelled.

"Good idea!"

But Atlas did nothing. Now they were just a dark speck, moving through gray.

Dan peered ahead. They were at the mouth of the harbor now. The ocean seemed roiling and savage. The cabin cruiser felt impossibly small. It was being tossed on the waves like a toy rubber duck, and Atlas just kept pushing the speed.

When they were out in the middle of the harbor, the thrum of the engine under Dan's feet stopped. There was nothing but the sound of the wind and rain, and the waves slapping against the hull.

Atlas had turned off the engine.

Dan's mouth went dry. He tried to swallow.

When Atlas turned back toward them, he was holding a gun.

CHAPTER 20

Singapore

The tropical heat of Singapore hit Nellie when they were still waiting in line at passport control. Once through the line and into the terminal, they moved through the crush at baggage claim. Sammy scanned the crowd. It had taken them a night and a day to reach Singapore, with stopovers in Los Angeles and Hong Kong, and Nellie felt sleep tugging at her eyelids. All she wanted was a cup of strong coffee. A donut wouldn't hurt, either.

"Shouldn't we find a taxi?" Nellie asked.

"Won't need one."

Men in dark suits and caps stood on one side, holding signs. Sammy found the one that said MOURAD.

"Have I mentioned that Uncle James is loaded?"

"Never turn down a chauffeur holding a sign," Nellie said. "One of my life rules."

The chauffeur drove through the city, past office buildings and down lovely boulevards. The roads had been washed by an early morning rain. Glittering tall buildings marched along wide streets. They passed through a business district, and suddenly they were in a quiet neighborhood of beautiful homes.

The driver turned down a street lined with palm trees. Nellie glimpsed stately homes behind a screen of lush greenery and flowering trees. The driver pulled into a long drive massed with blooming pink and yellow bushes.

A modern white house was at the end of the drive. A petite young woman stood in front, strikingly pretty in a yellow sleeveless dress, her black hair in a bun. As the car drew up, Nellie could see that woman was older than she appeared, middle-aged and gorgeous.

As soon as the car stopped, Sammy bounded out and into a hug.

Tiffany Chen held him at arm's length. "You get taller every time I see you. How are Darsh and Maya?"

"Fine, I guess. I haven't heard from them in a few days. Have you?" Nellie noted the anxiety in Sammy's voice.

Tiffany Chen shook her head. "They're probably spending all their time in the lab. Typical!"

"Aunt Tiff, I want you to meet Nellie Gomez. Nellie, this is Tiffany Chen."

"How do you do, Mrs. Chen," Nellie said, striving for her most formal manners in the midst of such elegance.

"Oh, call me Tiff." Tiff shook Nellie's hand. "I'm sure we'll be great friends. I've heard about you. You're rather a legend among the Cahills."

"Me?" Nellie was taken aback.

"The fearless Madrigal, Nellie Gomez," Tiff said. "Feats of incredible bravery. Got shot in the shoulder and the bullet was dug out without anesthetic, basically saved the world with the help of this kid here . . . Oh yes, Nellie, I've heard of you. Now come inside; James is in his office. I know he wants to talk to you two."

"As I told you on the phone, we think that the Outcast was operating in Singapore until recently," Sammy said as they walked up the stairs to the front door.

"At first I thought the Outcast takeover was just a joke," Tiff said, her lips pressing together. "It all sounded so ridiculous. I thought it would last a few hours at most. The Cahills have always battled and sniped at each other. It's why we got out. Tired of the infighting."

"I didn't realize you were outside of the Cahill circle now," Sammy said. "Uncle James set up the stronghold here."

"Yes, James was very involved for a time, but that was several years ago. Before the Clue hunt, really. We had quarrels with Bae Oh's leadership, and we fell away."

Nellie nodded. She couldn't blame them for having

problems with Bae Oh. He was a ruthless despot, safely in prison now.

The atrium was open and airy, with skylights for illumination. White sofas ran along one whole wall, and bright paintings were splashes of color on the walls. Fans revolved overhead. Exquisite orchids sat in blue-and-white pots. Floor-to-ceiling windows gave a view of green gardens, flowers, a tennis court, and a turquoise pool.

"Sammy, you're here!" A young girl raced toward them, her ponytail streaming out behind her. She looked like a miniature adult in a navy blazer and skirt and white shirt and tie.

"Mabel!" Sammy bent down to give the girl a hug.

"My daughter, Mabel Rose," Tiff said with an indulgent smile. "Mabel, this is Nellie Gomez."

"How do you do," Mabel said. Her tone was polite despite the fact that Sammy had her in a headlock and was giving her a noogie.

"I used to babysit for this squirt," Sammy said. "We used to catch lizards in the garden."

"Are you here to investigate what's going on?" Mabel asked. "Is there going to be another Clue hunt? Because I'm old enough now to join in. I'm eleven."

Tiff frowned. "You know the rules, darling. You are not to be involved in Cahill affairs. James!"

A handsome man in shirtsleeves hurried toward Sammy. James shook Sammy's hand, then hugged him. "Sammy, I was so glad to hear you were coming. I have been monitoring Ekat chatter for the past twenty-four hours. I'm shocked at how many Ekats are listening to this madman."

"We heard the Outcast called a meeting in Singapore and some high-level Cahills were invited," Sammy said.

James nodded. "I heard this, too."

"We were not invited," Tiff said. "They know how loyal we are to Grace's memory."

"Did you know Grace well?" Nellie asked.

"Not intimately. But she was a force." Tiff smiled. "A role model for me. She was so strong. And how are Amy and Dan? I heard they left the family."

"They're back," Nellie said. "They're helping to stop the Outcast. My kiddos would never let down the family."

"I had no idea they were back. That's good to hear."

"I think there's got to be someone who will talk about the Outcast," Mabel said. "I have a suggestion!"

Tiff turned, her displeasure evident. "Mabel, this is not for you to concern yourself with. You have your studies. Your Chinese tutor will be here in thirty minutes, and you must practice your violin first. You have a tennis lesson at four. You can catch up with Sammy at dinner."

"Yes, Mother," Mabel said. She gave one last reluctant look at Sammy before heading out of the room.

"I've used every contact in Southeast Asia," James went on. "The next step is the other Ekat strongholds."

"If you could wrangle an invitation for me to visit, it would be terrific," Sammy said.

"Sammy, I'm overjoyed to see you, but I have to admit, I'm worried," Tiff said. "Can't you leave the investigating to James? I heard what the Outcast is planning. He sounds ruthless, maybe crazy. This could be dangerous. I . . ." She shot a quick, nervous look at James. "Today, I thought I was being followed."

"What?" James exploded. "And you didn't tell me?"

She put a hand on her husband's arm. "I think you're confusing me with some kind of fragile flower. No one is going to get to me."

"Of course. You're more than a match for anyone." James softened as he put his hand over hers. "I would never underestimate you. But we all need to be on alert."

Tiff nodded. "That's why I think Sammy and Nellie should relax and see what you can discover. But first, let's give our guests a chance to rest. They've had a long flight. Sammy, Nellie, let me show you to your rooms."

They followed Tiff down quiet corridors to the back of the house, where they passed through a courtyard to a guest cottage. A suite of bedrooms led off a private sitting room. Tiff left them, suggesting they rest and join them for dinner at seven.

Nellie couldn't imagine resting. She dropped her pack in her room and wandered back to the sitting room. She poured a glass of iced tea from a frosty pitcher sitting in a bowl of ice. The tea tasted minty and cool.

She opened the French doors to a small patio. The cool greens of the trees were brilliant against the blue sky. A colorful bird dipped and soared above, then came to rest on the branch of a tree.

"Sammy!" Nellie called. "I think I see a parrot!"

"It's a kingfisher." The voice came from behind a bush.

Nellie peeked around the bush. Mabel sat on the grass barefoot, a violin tucked under her chin. She played a few notes. "There are three hundred and seventy-six bird species in Singapore," she said. "Some studies say more." She played another string of notes. One of them screeched.

Nellie winced.

Mabel smiled. "I know. Don't quit my day job, right?"

"Listen, kiddo, I've lived through Dan Cahill practicing the trombone. This is nothing."

"Music to your ears!"

"Well, I wouldn't go that far," Nellie teased. Mabel grinned, and just like that, they were friends. Nellie picked up a blossom that had fallen in the grass and twirled it in her fingers. "You were about to say something inside when your mom cut you off."

"I'm not allowed to get into anything Cahill related. Of course, they think I'm too young for everything. They're so protective. In my business *constantly*. All these gigantic windows in the house? It's so they always know what I'm up to."

"They just want to protect you."

"Dur. I'm eleven, but I'm not an idiot."

Nellie turned away to hide her smile. "Why don't you tell me now what you wanted to say?"

Mabel swung the violin off her shoulder and pointed the bow at Nellie. "If I was going to start a conspiracy, I'd start with the people who are already outsiders."

"That's exactly right," Nellie agreed. "It would be great if we knew someone here in Singapore that the Outcast tried to recruit. . . ."

"I might." Mabel sawed away at the violin.

Nellie wanted to grab the violin and get the answer, but she knew better. Mabel was tired of being treated like a kid. "I'd love to know what you think."

Mabel stopped playing. "Bee Arnold," she said triumphantly. "She just moved here six months ago. Rumor is that she was a big Ekat. Mother gave her a welcome dinner, but I don't think anyone liked her. Then she sort of became this hermit. I think everybody forgot about her."

"Except maybe the Outcast," Nellie said.

"Exactly!" Mabel dug in her pocket and handed her a piece of paper. "Here's her address out in Punggol.

Take the MRT, it's the fastest way. Take the North East line all the way to the end. Now I have to do my homework." She took off running. "And don't tell my parents!" she tossed over her shoulder.

In the Punggol district, restaurants with enticing smells called to Nellie.

"*Popiah*," Sammy told her. "Vegetarian spring rolls. *Gado gado*," he said, pointing to someone eating in a sidewalk café. "One of my favorite salads. Vegetables, cucumber, steamed rice cakes in a spicy peanut sauce."

"It's no fair being in Singapore and not able to eat. It's like leading a horse to water and not letting him drink. It's like holding a lollipop out of a kid's reach. It's like locking Amy out of a library. It's like . . ." Nellie realized she was talking to empty air. Sammy was behind her, speaking to a guy at a street cart.

Sammy came back and handed her a bundle. "Here. *Goreng pisang*. Deep-fried banana fritters. This will hold you over. Plus I got directions."

"You are my superhero," Nellie said through a mouthful of deep-fried deliciousness.

Sammy turned down a causeway that ran along the bay. Nellie checked her GPS. "No wonder we're lost," she said. "The street isn't on the map."

Bee Arnold's street turned out to be a tiny, over-grown alley. The leafy branches of the trees met over their heads, creating a green tunnel they walked down. Nellie felt like she was underwater. They passed modest cottages painted in pretty pastels, tucked away behind little gardens.

Bee Arnold's house was blue with yellow shutters. Climbing vines covered the gate, and the door was painted a ravishing shade of pink. Nellie felt reassured by the pots of flowers on the porch.

"Lovely," Nellie whispered. "A double-crosser wouldn't spend all this time gardening and planting flowers, would they?"

They knocked on the front door. Nellie heard soft footsteps.

Dressed in a faded sundress and sandals, her red hair in a long braid, Sinead Starling opened the door.

"Ah," Nellie said. "I guess I was wrong."

CHAPTER 21

Sinead's shock was visible on her face, but she recovered quickly. "Nellie. This is a surprise."

"I'm sure it is," Nellie said. "Can we come in?"

Sinead turned and led the way inside. The last time Nellie had seen her had been over a year ago, after they'd discovered that Sinead had been the mole who'd betrayed them. Even though Amy had forgiven her and even offered her a place to stay on Grace's estate, Sinead had disappeared with her brothers, and nobody had particularly wanted to find her.

Nellie didn't particularly trust her now, either.

Ted Starling walked into the room, smiling. "I know that voice! Nellie!"

Nellie hurried over and hugged him. "It's so good to see you! You look fantastic." She was fond of Ted and was happy to see him looking so rested and healthy.

"You mean, besides the blind thing?" Ted grinned. "I'm great. Starting to see shadows and colors again.

The doctors say the trauma is healing slowly." Ted had lost his sight in the original Clue hunt due to an explosion.

"That is fantastic news." Nellie introduced Sammy to the Starlings.

"Ned is better, too," Ted said. "He gets those terrible headaches less and less."

"We're all better here," Sinead said quietly.

She led them through the bright living room and into a small sitting area off the kitchen. "We mostly hang out here," she explained.

"It's pretty," Nellie said. The lush garden bloomed with flowers, and she saw the blue glint of the sea. The house was decorated in shades of white and pale blue, except for a glass vase crowded with pink flowers. It was obvious that the Starlings had worked hard to create a peaceful home.

"It's remarkable, actually," Sinead said. "We're . . . happy."

It was true that Sinead looked different. Gone were the buttoned-up polo shirts and pressed trousers. She was dressed in a loose linen dress, and Nellie noted how she kicked off her sandals as soon as she sat down. Yes, this Sinead was much more relaxed than she remembered.

"Why are you calling yourself Bee Arnold?" Nellie asked.

Sinead's mouth twisted. "Isn't it a good name for a traitor?"

B. Arnold. Benedict Arnold. Nellie understood in a rush.

"So you exiled yourself here," she said.

Sinead glanced at her brother. "Amy forgave the unforgivable. That shouldn't make it harder, but it did. I just couldn't face anyone anymore."

"Ned and I were worried about Sinead," Ted explained. "She would hardly get out of bed. Ned and I were the ones to contact the Ekat network. We knew she needed to go far away. We all needed to start over. They arranged the false identities, the best doctors, even this house. They invited us to a fancy welcome dinner."

"Who is 'they'?" Sammy asked.

"Patricia Oh and a friend of hers," Ted said.

"A friend?" Nellie sat up. "Who?"

"We never met him," Ted said. "She called him Oh. We figured he was a relative. She'd say, 'Don't worry, Oh will take care of that!'"

"'Oh,' like her last name? Or 'O,' like an initial?" Nellie asked.

Ted frowned in a puzzled way. "I don't know, actually. I just assumed it was a relative, come to think of it."

"This dinner," Nellie said. "Where was it?"

"At some fancy house. I think their name was Chen."

Nellie gave a start, which she tried to conceal by readjusting her position on the sofa.

Sammy leaned forward. "Was 'O' at the dinner?"

Sinead shook her head. "I don't think he was invited. We've kept away from Patricia since then.

Frankly, I never liked her. There's something . . . off about her niceness. And she gave me a big pitch on getting involved in the Asian branch of the Ekats. She said I deserved a leadership position again. That she was prepared to back me all the way. I told her I wasn't interested, and she didn't take no for an answer."

"What do you mean? What did she say?"

"A lot of manipulative stuff," Sinead said. "About how I was justified in what I did. About how she was going to be the new branch leader and she needed people she could trust." She shook her head with a rueful smile. "And why would she think she could trust me? I betrayed my best friend."

"You did it to protect us," Ted said softly, but Sinead just shook her head.

"Have you heard about the Outcast?" Nellie asked. "Did Patricia ever mention him?"

Sinead shook her head. "I've never heard that name." She gave Nellie and Sammy a shrewd look. "Are you saying that it could be the 'O' Patricia was talking about?"

"Possibly," Nellie said. "Patricia has joined forces with someone called the Outcast and kicked Ian Kabra and Cara Pierce out of the mansion. The Outcast is in control, and he's set up a contest to test Cahill leadership."

Sinead looked genuinely shocked and concerned. "What about Amy? Is she okay?"

"She's fine," Nellie said shortly. She was a lioness

when it came to her kiddos. Sinead may have seemed different, but she wasn't about to trust her, either.

"You said Patricia didn't take no for an answer," Sammy said. "Did she contact you again?"

Sinead nodded. "Recently. Last month. She asked me to tea at the Raffles Hotel. I didn't want to go, but she insisted. She said she had important news. But actually she just wanted to pressure me to attend a meeting. She said others who had been wronged by Grace's grandchildren would be there. I told her I didn't feel that way anymore. She said that change was going to happen whether I liked it or not. It would be better to be with them than against them. She frightened me. I told her not to contact me anymore. I said I wouldn't do anything to betray Amy and Dan ever again. She was quite . . . nasty about it. There was an implied threat."

"Did she say anything else? Did she give you any names of others?"

Sinead shook her head. "I'm sorry."

"What about something that seemed small, or didn't make sense?" Sammy asked.

"Nothing." A spark of memory lit Sinead's face. "Just one thing. Probably nothing. I got there a bit late, and she was on the phone. I came up behind her and heard her say that the jet had taken off from Chicago with the package."

"Chicago," Nellie repeated. Not much to go on.

"It's a big city," Sammy said, echoing her thoughts. "Doesn't exactly narrow it down."

"Tell her what you told me last night," Ted said.

Sinead hesitated. "Ever since I said no to Patricia, I have this creepy feeling. Like my e-mails and phone are monitored. I took Ned to the doctor a few days ago, and I was sure I was being followed."

Nellie exchanged a glance with Sammy.

"Did anything else happen?" she asked Sinead.

Sinead shook her head. "Patricia was so vindictive. She said the Cahill family was in deep trouble. That Amy and Dan and now Ian had made so many mistakes. Children had destroyed it, and adults would put it back together again." She looked at Nellie directly. "I have to admit I've been worrying about it, thinking about maybe contacting Amy. I have no right to warn anybody, or to have anybody listen to me. But I've been there. I've felt resentment like that — so huge it takes over your life. I let it twist me into a creature who would stop at nothing to get revenge. I know what that's like, and I saw it in her."

"We just want to live quietly," Ted said.

Sinead twisted her hands. "We can't help you any more. Can you please go now?"

Nellie stood. "Thanks for talking to us. It was good to see you, Ted."

Sinead walked them toward the door. "Do me a favor? Tell Amy I wasn't part of this?"

"I'll tell her."

Sinead opened the door. "And tell her to be careful. Tell her . . ." Sinead bit her lip. "Tell her I'm afraid."

CHAPTER 22

Halifax Harbor, Nova Scotia

Ian stepped in front of Amy. He didn't look at the muzzle of the gun. He looked at Atlas's face. His cold eyes.

This wasn't a threat. He wasn't trying to scare them. This was real.

"Just a moment," Ian said. "We have a deal."

Atlas's lip curled. "Do you think I'd allow a bunch of kids to threaten me? Know my business?"

"We might know your business better than you do. We have reason to believe your ship is booby-trapped. When it gets into the harbor, it will explode."

"Right. And all the mermaids will drown, and the unicorns will save them. Kid, I don't have time for this. I run a billion-dollar operation, do you understand? You're in my way, and you know too much. All of you, kneel down. In a line, facing away from me. Hands on top of your heads."

He's going to execute us, one by one.

Ian could taste his own fear, acrid in his mouth. He

felt suddenly light-headed. Yet at the same time every-thing was so clear. Possibilities whipped through his head at lightning speed. He saw pitfalls and dangers and outcomes. None of them were good.

He could also feel his friends behind him, breathing, scared, ready. The unsteady pitch of the deck underneath his feet. The fog leaving droplets on his cheeks. Life was so big and so close, it seemed impossible that this could be happening.

Amy stood slightly behind him, muscles coiled, waiting for an opening. He knew she was ready to strike.

Ham was to his left. Dan's eyes were darting from the gun to the distance between him and Atlas. They were each ready to rush the guy with the gun.

Which was exactly what could get them all killed.

Ian had never been so afraid in his life. But he had just gone through every possibility in this scenario and rejected them all.

Except for one.

Atlas didn't know who he was dealing with. Not just kids, but trained, strong attackers. Amy was a black belt, and Hamilton could probably bench-press a car to protect his friends. Dan was fearless and quick. If Atlas killed Ian, that would give the others enough time to rush him, get the gun. They'd only have a second, maybe two, but that was all they needed, and Atlas would never expect kids to be that fast.

"I'm not kneeling down," he said.

Amy drew in a sharp breath.

"No, Ian," she breathed behind him. She knew what he was thinking.

He wasn't the self-sacrificing sort, but Atlas had placed him in that position.

Atlas swung the gun toward Ian's temple.

"Fine," he said. "You first."

He stared into Atlas's eyes. He saw no compassion, no mercy. Just a willingness to get the job done.

Behind Atlas's head, a freighter moved toward the harbor. Their boat was angled parallel. That meant the wake would hit them broadside.

Which would give him one last chance. If he could stall.

"Before you do, you should listen," Ian said. "We have absolute evidence that the ship is rigged to explode. I have it right on my phone. Let me show you. If you don't look, you'll regret it."

"I never regret anything," Atlas said. "And if the ship blows, no one can connect me with it."

"We can," Amy said.

"But you'll be dead, kid," Atlas said. He flourished the gun. "Didn't you get the memo?"

The wave hit. Ian had watched it come over Atlas's shoulder, rolling across the dark water. He was braced and ready. The boat lifted and pitched, and Atlas staggered.

It was all they needed.

Ian slammed into Atlas, aiming his hand in a lethal chop to the man's throat. Meanwhile, Amy went in close with a roundhouse kick right at Atlas's wrist. Ian could have sworn he heard the crack of bone, and Atlas howled. The gun went skittering on the deck and Dan dove for it. Hamilton crashed into a tottering Atlas with the full force of his body.

Dan threw the gun overboard. Atlas struggled to get clear of Hamilton. He broke free and barreled down the steps into the cabin. Ian realized he must have another weapon down there.

"Let's go!" Ian shouted. He hit the winch that lowered the dinghy down and flipped the ladder over the side. "Move!"

Amy climbed down the ladder and threw herself in. Dan followed. "Ham, come on!" Ian shouted. He wouldn't leave this deck until Ham was safely in the dinghy.

Ham had one foot over the railing as Atlas charged back up to the deck, holding a gun.

The crack of the gun exploded over Ian's head as Ham scooped up the anchor and threw it. It connected with Atlas's head, and he collapsed onto the deck with a clunk.

Ham vaulted off the railing and into the dinghy. Ian was right behind him.

"NOW!" Ian shouted, and with a mighty heave, Hamilton pushed them off.

The current drove them out, skimming over the chop. Amy shipped the oars and began to row as hard as she could. The fog wrapped around them.

"We made it," Ian said.

The blast of a ship's horn made them jump.

"We're in the middle of a shipping channel with fog rolling in and a storm coming," Dan said through chattering teeth. "And the current is pulling us out into the North Atlantic. But you can't have everything."

"We all did splendidly back there," Ian said. "Now let's get ourselves to shore. Amy, I have the greatest confidence in your muscles, but perhaps Hamilton should row."

"Which direction?" Hamilton asked.

Ian looked around. He could see nothing. No lights, no buoys, no stars. The fog was so thick now it obscured every landmark. They could no longer distinguish the sea from the sky. It was all gray. Thick, impenetrable gray, with the cold black sea all around them and darkness falling.

"That is indeed the question," he said.

Which was exactly when a loud blast from a ship's horn reverberated across the water. Ian felt it as pressure in his ears and chest. Now they could feel the vibration of the great powerful engines.

The massive gray ship emerged from the fog straight at them.

CHAPTER 23

"There it is!" Dan shouted as another earsplitting blast ripped through the air. "Ham! ROW!"

"Hang on!" Ian shouted.

The gray mass looked more like a building than a ship, or a gigantic tsunami made of metal. It bore straight at them.

Terror blasted through Amy as the wall of the ship headed for them, tons of steel and mighty power.

Hamilton's arms moved like pistons, each stroke going deep in the water, pulling them away from the ship's path. He kept them slicing through the water against incredible odds, just from the power of his arms and sheer will. The dinghy moved, incredibly slowly it seemed to Amy, but it moved, scudding across the water. They could be pulling out to sea instead of toward land but it didn't matter, they had to get away from the massive ship, out of the shipping lanes, anywhere but where they were and with what could happen. She pictured the ship slicing into them, the boat splintering, their bodies tossed into the cold sea. . . .

We've got to make it, we've got to . . .

Horn blasting, fog swirling, Ham's desperate panting, his lungs on fire . . .

They cleared it by only yards.

Amy felt the immensity of the ship as the whole of it revealed itself as it slid past.

"Get ready for the wake!" Ham cried. "It could swamp us! We've got to head into it!"

A wall of water was coming at them. The boat heaved up, up, up, then slammed down. Water cascaded into the boat. They all screamed in terror as another wave hit.

"Hang on!" Ham howled, wiping water out of his eyes.

They hung on as the boat heaved and quivered and the water roiled around them. Amy was afraid the boat would break apart.

Then there was nothing but gray water and fog, and the slippery edge of the boat against her fingers. They rocked on midsize waves. The cold water was up to their ankles.

"Dan, Amy, start bailing," Ian said in a clipped tone that rang with desperation. "Dan, use your hands. Amy, take this." Ian took off his boot and handed it to her.

"You'll freeze!"

"Better than drowning." Ian took off his other boot.

Hamilton started to row again. "At least we know the ship is heading for the harbor."

"But we're still in the shipping lane!" Amy said. "We have to go right or left."

"Wait, I have one piece of good news." Dan's voice sliced through the gloom. "I grabbed a phone on the way out." He held up a phone.

"Text Cara and see if she can get our position," Ian said.

"And is there a flashlight app on that?" Amy asked. "We can use the strobe."

Even though there was no longer a wake, the seas were choppy. The sleeting rain dripped down their necks, and soon they were all shaking with cold. Occasionally, a wave would splash over the edge of the dinghy. It was a small boat built for trips from the pier to a mooring. Not for this. Not for the choppy waters of an outer harbor. If they got swept out to sea . . .

Don't think about it. Concentrate on bailing. On rowing.

"Did Cara answer us?" Amy asked Dan.

Dan paused in his bailing to check the phone. "She's pinpointed our position!" He handed the phone to Ian.

Amy rubbed her hands together. She felt frozen and scared. They were bailing as fast as they could, but it didn't feel as though they were making a difference.

"We're not going to make it unless you BELIEVE it!" Ham roared as he rowed. "There is no such thing as 'can't' in the Holt universe!"

"Cara's given me compass headings." Ian accessed the app. "Ten degrees to the right, Ham. Steer us home!"

With Ian directing and bailing, they made slow progress. Ian squinted off to his right. "I think I see a light!" he shouted. "Look!"

Amy squinted. The fog was shredding into patchy areas. It lay more thickly on the water, but she was just beginning to see a shape.

"It's land!" she cried. "I see lights! I see them! That way!"

From across the dark water a light blinked three times.

"Look!" Dan shouted. He engaged the strobe on the phone and signaled back, holding the phone high. After a moment the lights blinked three times again.

"Woo-hoo!" Ham screamed. "All right, you land-lubbers, we're going to BEACH THIS THING!"

When they heard the dinghy scrape over the rocks, they crawled out. They collapsed on a rocky beach.

"I thought we were done for," Amy said, her mouth against a slimy rock. After a few seconds she raised her head. "I hear . . . traffic. What a beautiful sound!"

She turned and looked at Dan. He appeared pale, exhausted, his hands gripping the sand.

"I'm sorry," she said softly. "I got us back into this."

Dan struggled to sit up, his eyes on Ian and Hamilton as they stumbled up the beach toward a parking lot.

"C'mon, guys!" Hamilton called.

Lights flashed as a car door opened, and Cara and Jonah tumbled out. Cara hurtled herself at Ian and hugged him. Jonah clapped his arms around Hamilton.

"Truth?" Dan asked. "We both know we couldn't live with ourselves if we turned our backs on them."

He rose and put his hand out to help Amy. She put her icy hand in his, and he pulled her to her feet. She was startled at his power. When had her baby brother become as tall as she was? When had he developed this wiry strength?

"After this—" she started, but he interrupted.

"There is no after this," he said. "There's only now. There's only stopping it."

Amy forgot, sometimes, that her jokey brother had a way of seeing the world in terms of what was essential. She had a tendency to overcomplicate things. She relied on him for how he could lay things out, sum it all up in a simple truth.

There was only now. There was only stopping this. Yes.

"We have to get it back," she said. "All of it. Grace's house, the family."

Dan's face tightened. There had been times when Amy had been afraid of that look. Afraid that Dan was too young to look so hard.

Now she had to admit how much she relied on his toughness.

"Oh, we'll get it back," Dan said, his eyes glittering. "That's a promise."

Rain drummed against the windshield of the rental car. Cara kept the motor running. She'd been blasting the heat, so that the car was toasty warm. It calmed their shivering, but not their nerves.

"The ship must be coming into port now," Ian said. "Halifax could blow sky-high."

"So. Which way should I go?" Cara asked, her hands on the wheel.

Nobody said what they all were surely thinking. If they were too late, shouldn't they be *leaving*? Should she head to the airport?

A sudden gust of wind shook the car. Amy glanced from one pale face to another. She knew that they all felt as she did. They couldn't leave the city. Not even if there was just a minuscule chance to save it.

"We need to go to the police," Cara said. "Even if nobody believes us."

"It could be the only option left," Amy agreed quietly.

"But the Outcast said no outsiders," Dan pointed out.

Nobody said anything for a long minute. They were trapped.

"As Dan would say, I blew it," Ian said. "I over-played my hand. I threatened Atlas, and we all came close to getting shot."

"Don't beat yourself up about it, bro," Jonah said. "Focus on the problem."

"You didn't leave that boat until you knew we were all safe," Amy said to Ian. "That's leadership. You were willing to be *killed* to save us."

"What?" Cara asked. She whipped around to look at Ian in the backseat. "What did you do?"

"He basically walked right up to a guy with a gun and said, 'Shoot me first,'" Hamilton said. "Bravest thing I'd ever seen, dude."

"Or the stupidest!" Cara exclaimed.

"I know I often fall into the 'stupid' category with you, Cara," Ian said, his face flushing. "But in this case, it was necessary."

Amy almost groaned aloud. *No, Ian! Cara was try-ing to let you know she cares about you!* He could be so *clueless* when it came to human emotion!

"Now," Ian continued, "I agree that we need to bring in the authorities. I just don't think we're going to get far walking into a police station. They won't believe us, and it will take more time than we've got to establish that we're not crazy pranksters. We're not dealing with days anymore. We could be dealing with *minutes.* This storm has pushed up the timeline. The ship is in port. We have to do something. But who's going to believe a bunch of kids?"

"That question seems to come up a depressing amount when you're a Cahill," Dan agreed.

Jonah suddenly started to wiggle in his seat, trying to get his fingers down into the front pocket of his jeans. He fished out a business card and held it up. "I have a way. Head for the pier."

CHAPTER 24

It took all of Jonah's persuasiveness and star power to get Bill Hannigan to agree to meet them. It was a busy night at the port, and Mr. Hannigan was in charge of making sure every ship met its berth safely. Dressed in a slicker and hard hat, he checked his watch impatiently as Jonah and the others arrived.

They huddled against the rain as Mr. Hannigan listened to Jonah's explanation of how he'd been researching at a pier and overheard the information about setting off an explosion on the *Aurora*.

Hannigan checked the manifest. "It's refrigerator parts from Suriname," he said. "Pipes, liners, coils."

"But the ship's captain was arrested three years ago for illegal weapons trafficking," Amy said, showing him the article on her tablet. "He works for James Atlas."

"And I heard the guy mention his name," Jonah said.

"I know who Atlas is," Mr. Hannigan said with a deep frown. He looked out at the pier, where the

Aurora was docked. "Haven't cleared the ship yet. The crew is still aboard."

"I guarantee you, Mr. Hannigan," Jonah said. "Something funky and explosive is on that boat."

"Ship," Mr. Hannigan corrected, but his gaze was hard as he stared at the *Aurora*.

"What are you going to do, sir?" Ian asked. "There really isn't any time to waste."

"The thing is," Mr. Hannigan said, "doing my job is as much about instincts as your job is, Jonah." He spoke into a walkie-talkie. "Security, I have a level five alert. Yes, you heard me correctly. Meet me on the deck of the *Aurora*. Now."

They found Atlas with the captain in the wheelhouse. Atlas wore a bloody bandage on his head and an expression of deadly rage when he saw Ian, Amy, Dan, and the others walk in with Mr. Hannigan.

"Bump your head, Atlas?" Mr. Hannigan asked.

"Do I know you?" Atlas said coolly.

"You're about to."

Atlas flicked his gaze to the group. "You're listening to children's stories?"

"None of your business." He turned to his two security officers. "Detain them," he said curtly, and suddenly the executive in the gray suit they'd met the day before turned into an action hero. He began to snap orders, ignoring the captain's bluster and Atlas's threats.

"This is legitimate cargo, and you are wasting everyone's time," Atlas said. "You'll be sorry you did this." He said the words lightly. He was a man who didn't need to threaten. Just his presence there was enough.

Atlas took a step toward Hannigan, just a half step. His voice was low. "Moving cargo is what I do. Delays cost me. And I'd pay a great deal to avoid it. That's why I have friends in high places."

A bribe. A threat.

Amy felt the charge between the two men. What sickened her was that of the two of them, Atlas was far more powerful. He had billions of dollars behind him. Hannigan was a good man in a tough job.

She'd seen a whole lot of injustice in the world in the past few years. People who suffered, people who died. People who got power and didn't deserve it. People who got pushed around. *Life isn't fair*, her math teacher Mr. Alessi used to say when they'd moaned about a surprise quiz. How could she, that twelve-year-old Amy sitting in class, worried about a quiz, have known how deeply true that was?

"That sounded like you are bribing a port official," Hannigan said. He spoke into the walkie-talkie. "Search every corner of this ship."

Atlas looked at Amy. "You're dead, you know," he

told her. He said it as though they were having a conversation. "I don't care if you're a kid."

She gave him a cool glance. "I don't care if you're a criminal. Look me up when you get out of jail."

Much later, they stood on the pier as Atlas and the captain were loaded into a vehicle. Snow swirled in the lights. Atlas and the captain had been arrested on at least five charges having to do with bribery, violation of international law, arms trafficking . . . As Hannigan said, "I threw the book at them. And it's a very large book.

"Here's the thing," Hannigan said, turning up his collar against the snow. "The ship wasn't going to blow up. We know that for sure. You got that part wrong, but I'm grateful for what you got right. They were running mortars and automatic weapons to Suriname. It's enough to put them both away for a while." He cocked his head at Jonah. "See? We *do* get drama here occasionally."

"Word," Jonah said.

But Jonah looked as worried as the rest of them. They'd been wrong about the *Aurora*. But that didn't mean the city was safe. It just meant that their best shot had fizzled.

"Atlas made a lot of threats against you," Amy said.

"Part of the job," Hannigan said. "And it's in my blood. Both my father and grandfather worked on the piers. My great-grandfather was working the morning they got news that the *Titanic* went down. He was one of the men sent out from Halifax to search for passengers. Brought them back here to bury them."

Dan half turned to focus on Hannigan. "*Titanic* passengers? Buried here?"

"Sure," Hannigan said. "One hundred and fifty souls were brought here and buried. Most of them out in Fairview Cemetery. It's worth a visit. It makes you really feel the tragedy of that disaster."

"'In the Maritimes you'll find the crosses,'" Dan said.

"Exactly."

Dan looked thunderstruck. He stuck out his hand and shook Hannigan's heartily. "Thank you for believing us tonight. Best of luck!"

"Thanks," Hannigan replied, smiling a little at Dan's abruptness. "I'd better get back to my office. Make sure all the ships are safely berthed."

He said his good-byes and walked off. Immediately, Amy turned to Dan.

"What did you just think of?" she demanded.

"We got it all wrong!" Dan cried. "Totally!" He recited the poem. "'A collision caused the terrible losses / In the Maritimes you'll find the crosses.' He *was* talking about the *Titanic*! All of the rest of the poem fits, too. It happened in the middle of the night, so people were in their pajamas . . ."

"Wait a second. What about maiming and blindness?" Amy asked. " 'On Mont Blanc rests the ones to blame / Oh, to maim, blind, and kill, and have no shame!' Nobody was maimed or blinded in the *Titanic* disaster."

"That part isn't about the *Titanic*," Dan declared. "It's about us, Amy! Where were we when the Outcast took over the mansion? *On Mont Blanc* — the real one, the mountain! He was letting us know that he knew exactly where we were and what we were doing."

"But you didn't blind or kill anyone," Cara said.

"No." Ian's voice was quiet. "Amy and Dan didn't. But Ted Starling was blinded in that explosion in Philadelphia. Ned Starling was maimed, in a way. He never really recovered. If you were a crazy lunatic, you could blame them . . . blame all the Madrigals, I guess. Because of what the hunt did to Cahills."

Amy put a hand to her mouth. "He's blaming us for everything. That's why he took over."

"Do you see what this means? The city is safe!" Dan exclaimed.

"But something else is going to happen," Cara said. "And now we might be too late. We wasted so much time! Two and a half days! There's less than three days left, and we haven't figured out the target."

Jonah had been busy working his phone. He drew in a breath. "I've got the target," he said. "Look."

He held out his phone. They all crowded in to scan the news report.

BREAKING NEWS

***TITANIC II* MAIDEN VOYAGE**
Defying icebergs, replica sails to Antarctica
Notables on board include sponsor Peter Zimmer, richest man in the world; Nobel Prize winners; and Oscar-winning actress Janelle Beladon. *Ship sails from Argentina on March 1.* >

• Cahills at it again >

"That's tomorrow," Amy said.

CHAPTER 25

Singapore

Mabel Rose Chen was a perfect daughter. She knew this because everybody said it.

Mabel is the perfect daughter. Her grades! Her music! Her sports! Her manners! Her hair! You must be so proud.

She didn't want to be perfect. She wanted to be *necessary.*

Her parents had raised three sons ahead of Mabel. She was the surprise. Her brothers were all in college. She was the afterthought. For a while, her nickname had been "Tag" for "tagalong." Until she asked them to stop.

Her parents were probably tired of raising kids. Tired of overseeing and reminding and prodding. That must be why they were sending her away to boarding school in Switzerland for the summer. They *said* it was to perfect her French. Mabel knew they wanted to get rid of her.

Something was wrong in the house. Mabel had

always been the youngest one in the room, and that had taught her how to listen. How to become invisible in a room full of people talking.

Her father had been up since four A.M. Her mother had taken three aspirins and snapped at Mabel when she asked what was for dinner. Now they were in the study with the door closed.

One of the unbreakable rules of the household was this: The Chen children had to stay out of Cahill business until they were twenty-one.

The thing about being a perfect daughter was that nobody suspected that you might not be so perfect. That maybe you were fascinated by the fact that you belonged to this powerful family, and maybe you weren't so great at violin or tennis or French, but you were very, very good at spying.

Mabel tiptoed to her mother's office. She had guessed her password long ago. What would it hurt if she went back and looked at the Ekat chatter from the past few weeks? And had a peek at some e-mails? She'd already done her homework.

She booted up and started to read.

After a few minutes, her heart began to pound.

She had to get up and walk around the room to get calm.

Then she went back to reading.

"I know what you're thinking," Sammy said as they left the alley and headed to the main road. "The Chens gave that dinner, and sure, it looks suspicious. But it was a welcome dinner for a fellow Ekat, so of course they invited Patricia. It doesn't mean they know the Outcast."

"I'm not thinking anything," Nellie answered. "We're just gathering information." But a tiny tendril of suspicion had taken root.

"We have a more immediate problem," Sammy said. "I think we're being followed."

"Who?"

"I don't know. It's a feeling on the back of my neck. I keep looking in shop windows and just missing something out of the corner of my eye. Just now I turned and someone quickly stepped into a food stall. Let's keep moving."

Nellie knew better than to look back. It was now close to six in the evening, and the street was crowded. She'd been walking without noticing anything, her head still focused on the scant information Sinead had given them, trying to extract a lead from the tangle. Now her nerves jumped to high alert.

Sammy picked up the pace. "You see that bus ahead? Let's jump on."

"Let's just get in line," Nellie said. "I want to flush whoever it is out."

People pressed against them as they approached the bus stop. Nellie took her sunglasses off and pretended to polish them. She looked around her, keeping her face down.

It was impossible to tell if someone was really on their trail. Food stalls had opened, and people were spilling out of buildings, heading to cafés before going home, or lining up for buses. It was a warm, lovely evening, and people were strolling, enjoying the air.

The bus lumbered to a stop. People shuffled forward. The bus was completely jammed, and some tried to press themselves aboard.

The doors slammed shut, the aisles full. The bus took off smoothly, leaving several people on the sidewalk.

"Rush hour in Singapore," a man said next to her. He shrugged. "What can you do? Now I'm going to miss meeting my friend." He gave them an easygoing smile. "He'll just have to start without me. Unless . . . you know, taxis are expensive, but we could split the fare. Where are you going? I'm in the Colonial District."

There was no way Nellie was getting into a car with a random guy. He looked like any normal person, a little tired after a long day, dressed casually in shorts and sandals. But all her senses were on alert. She fanned herself with her hand, but all the while she studied him carefully.

"Thanks, but we're not too far. I think we'll walk," she said. "Such a beautiful day. Nice meeting you."

They started to walk off. "I don't trust him," Nellie murmured. "Let's see if he follows us."

"Isn't the idea to get *away* from the guy?" Sammy asked.

"I want to see if I can get a photo," she said. "Cara can run it through her ID software."

As they turned at the next corner, she glanced in a shop window. Was he back there? She saw the flash of a white shirt, a tanned arm.

They hurried down the road and crossed into a green park. Sammy checked his phone. "If we walk straight through here, we'll come to an MRT station. We can catch a train back. I don't know if we're being followed, but I know how strict mealtimes are at the Chens'."

Nellie gave a quick look back, but she didn't spot the man who had spoken to them at the bus stop. What if he'd just been a normal, friendly guy?

Near a fountain with squealing children, she saw a different man enter the park. He looked like every other tourist, in a white shirt and a Panama hat that shadowed his features. Had she noticed him before on the street? Something in the way he moved made her take a second look. She flashed back to the busy street. He'd been the pedestrian munching on a sweet from the vendor. Now as he walked, she noted a coiled energy about him that he was trying to disguise with an ambling stride.

Too far away to get a photo, and the hat shadowed

his face. Nellie suddenly felt a prick of foreboding. She'd learned to trust her instincts.

"Let's go this way." She pulled Sammy off the path. If they cut through this grove of trees, it should bring them closer to the train station.

Within a few steps, it was as though they'd plunged into a deep tropical forest. The trees were planted thickly here, and the branches shut out the last of the light and cut off the sounds of the park. Nellie could hear some children playing a game, but the sound seemed far away. They were alone. It seemed as though nobody in Singapore ever strayed off the neat pathways.

Except . . .

Nellie stopped.

"Sammy, did you hear that? Footsteps?"

"No." Sammy cocked his head. "Nothing."

They walked again. This time, when she heard the rustle she stopped and whirled around.

Nothing.

She reached for Sammy's hand. She suddenly regretted striking off the path. They continued to walk, faster this time. The rustling continued.

"Hey there," someone crooned.

But there was no one there.

Sammy squeezed her hand, pulling her along.

"Nel-lie . . ." The voice sent a chill of fear through her. Sammy gave her a startled glance.

"Let's get out of here," he said in a low voice.

They were walking fast now, almost running. Nellie could hear the footsteps, but she couldn't tell where they were, or where the voice was coming from. The trees cast deep green shadows. Was that rustling a bird in the leaves, or their pursuer?

She didn't want to be scared. She'd been in tough situations before. This was just a voice.

A voice that *knew her.*

Then suddenly, the man in the hat was ahead of them, only yards away.

"Nosy girls should be careful."

Nellie was about to fling out a reply when she was distracted by a flash of silver. The man was spinning a steel rod around and around in his hand, so fast she only saw a blur. The rod was attached to a thick metal ring on his third finger. His pinkie finger was missing a joint.

She had time to notice those things, but no time to react before his hand flicked, and the rod turned out to be a foot-long spear hurtling cleanly through the air. It passed between her and Sammy and thwacked into a tree. It had been so close she'd felt it tickle the hair near her ear. If she had turned, had even flinched . . .

"Relax. If I'd wanted to hit you, I would have."

Sammy surged toward the man.

"SAMMY, NO!" Nellie shouted. She leaped forward and grabbed him with both hands. "No," she whispered. "No." She saw the second weapon in the man's hand, twirling.

"Don't even think of it, boyfriend. Next time I won't miss."

Sammy went still, but she heard his harsh breathing.

"Just a warning, this time," he said softly. "Go home, *kiddos*. I mean, all the way home. Back to the States. Or next time, it will be in your back."

CHAPTER 26

Ushuaia, Argentina

"Ushuaia is the southernmost city on the globe," Cara said. She'd done a ton of research on the plane. "It's the main jumping-off point for Antarctica, even though that means you have to go through Drake Passage, the most treacherous water in the world. It's this bottleneck at the tip of South America, around Cape Horn. Ships used to founder and sink there, and it's still notoriously dangerous."

"Look at it this way—it can't be worse than Halifax Harbor in a dinghy," Dan said.

Hamilton nudged Dan. "Good one."

Cara hadn't known Hamilton Holt for as long as the others, but she was always grateful for his cheerfulness. They had flown to the bottom of the world, and they all felt like zombies with duffel bags. Their bags were stuffed with fleece, boots, and waterproof gear they'd purchased locally in hopes they'd be able to get aboard.

They'd taken off from Halifax in a snowstorm and flown all night, with a blurred stopover in Chile. Hamilton had woken up momentarily, heard the word *Chile*, and mumbled, "I like mine with onions." The gang hadn't let him forget it.

"Thanks, Onions," Dan said.

"We have two and a half days before disaster strikes," Cara said.

"Must you keep repeating the deadline?" Ian asked.

"Yes," Cara said. Ian had been cool and distant since last night. Cara had concluded that he was an idiot. Even though he'd been incredibly brave, he'd also brushed her off when she'd been concerned about him. Just when she tried to show him she cared, he got all stiff and Brit-fuff-fuff.

So, she was going to play it cool with Ian Kabra, keep her head, and wait for her heart to catch up.

"Well, we're finally pointed in the right direction," Amy said. "As far south as you can get."

"This wasn't what I thought Argentina would look like," Hamilton said. "I was hoping to see horses galloping across the pampas. Even though I'm not sure what *pampas* even are."

"Grasslands," Cara said. "And they're a bit farther north."

Cara liked this bustling small city that curled around a deep blue harbor. The city was cupped by snowy mountain peaks. It was chilly and sunny, with colorful flowers blooming in windowsills and planted in grassy squares.

It was an upside-down world. It was March first, but that meant autumn in Antarctica. The summer research stations would be closing down, the scientists heading back to their home countries. The long Antarctic winter was around the corner. She'd learned that March was at the very tail end of Antarctic cruises—the season ran from November to March, with most cruises taking place during December and January, during the Antarctic summer. The *Titanic II* was an icebreaker, however, and was going to forge into the harbors of Antarctica and catch the very last of the good weather.

At least that was the plan.

They walked toward the harbor, crossing a plaza underneath a snapping light blue Argentine flag. The harbor was crowded with expedition ships alongside fishing boats and one gigantic cruise liner.

They stood on the sidewalk, duffels in their hands, scanning the pier. It was clear which boat was the *Titanic II*, even without reading the gilt letters on the stern. It was bright white and navy, with polished mahogany railings, and had attracted a crowd on the pier who stared up at its magnificence. People were pulling up in hired cars and SUVs, and crew members in snappy white uniforms were hurrying down to escort them and handle the luggage.

Hamilton gave a low whistle. "She's a beauty," he said.

"The ship has been booked solid for a year," Amy said. "Peter Zimmer is a *Titanic* fanatic, but he also runs a nonprofit foundation, and so he merged his two interests into this one ship to raise awareness. There's a mix of billionaires, scientists, a movie star who calls herself an environmentalist, and a very lucky group of seventeen high school science students from La Jolla, California, who Zimmer invited on the cruise."

"Zimmer says the ship combines the opulence of the first *Titanic* along with cutting-edge green technology," Cara added. "It's running on biofuels, and he's aiming for zero impact on the environment. Plus, he's replicating the meals of the first *Titanic* voyage and he's copied all the silver and plates and tablecloths."

Ian glanced over at the photographers clustered at the foot of the gangway. "No journalists once they get under way," he noted, "but they're to be given a tour of the ship while in port. That might give us a chance to sneak aboard, but they'll most likely be checking credentials very closely."

"So we don't have a plan," Dan said.

"Not until we scope it out," Amy answered. "How many passengers?" she asked Cara.

"About a hundred," Cara said. "Plus crew. Considerably less than the *Titanic*. It was the largest ship in the world at the time. There were about two thousand passengers and crew, I think. Less than half survived."

"Seven hundred and thirteen survivors," Dan said, because he was cursed with having random facts embedded in his brain forever. "That means about thirty percent survived. They had enough lifeboats for only half, and many of them didn't make it on. Some lifeboats weren't even full! At first they were afraid to lower them and thought they might split if they were at capacity. It was just stupid."

"The captain kept the ship at full power even though there were icebergs in the vicinity," Amy said. "It was common practice; nobody thought an iceberg could sink a ship. The ship was the most expensive ever built and believed to be unsinkable."

"It had sixteen watertight compartments that could be sealed off," Dan said. "It could survive four being disabled. The iceberg destroyed five."

"The unsinkable became sinkable," Amy said.

"The same reliance on technology that this *Titanic* has," Ian said. "So, based on historical record, I'd say we'd be foolish to think this ship can't blunder into disaster just as well."

Amy gazed out at the sea. "It was such an unbelievable tragedy at the time. The ship took almost three hours to sink. That's a lot of time for people to know that they were facing death. The husbands had to say good-bye to their wives and children and send them into lifeboats . . . and of course the first-class passengers got a crack at the lifeboats first. So all those third-class passengers and crew knew they were going to drown. There were a thousand people still aboard when the ship went down."

Cara shivered. "What kind of monster would wish that kind of disaster on the world again? And why? Just to prove a point? He's crazy."

"He might be," Amy said. "But he might be after something we haven't even figured out yet."

"Like what?" Dan asked.

"I don't know," Amy said. "But look at us. We're busy trying to save people. What is the Outcast doing?"

Ian nodded. "Exactly what I've been thinking. But he's given us no choice. We have to keep going."

Cara nodded. "We can't let it happen again. If the *Titanic II* sinks, prominent scientists will go down with it. The science of climate change will be set back for decades. Plus the world's foremost authorities on emperor penguins, volcanology, meteorites, and seals."

"Not to mention the president's adviser on the environment and a winner of the Nobel Peace Prize," Ian said.

"And the star of *Explosive Action: The Movie*," Jonah put in. "Hey, just saying. It's the maiden voyage. BOB. Bigwigs on board."

"And seventeen science nerds," Hamilton added as the high school students walked by, talking excitedly and pointing.

They fell silent as they watched the students. Cara felt something happen in her chest, and then her throat, which meant she was about to humiliate herself by tearing up. She had been trained not to cry by her father, who used to make a clown face and say *Look at the 'ittle crybaby* while her brother Galt jeered at her. No. She didn't cry. Not ever.

It was just that they all looked so . . . excited and happy. She couldn't get the image of passengers on the original *Titanic* out of her head. Standing on a freezing deck while it slanted underneath their feet and the crowds frantically looked for places in lifeboats that weren't there . . .

She looked around at the gang. She saw the same thoughts flickering on their faces. She trusted this group. She'd seen them in action. So, no way would this ship go down.

Two young men with beards and backpacks passed them, dressed in bright yellow parkas.

"Scientists," Jonah guessed.

"Rollo never showed up in the lobby," one of them said as they passed. "Said he was waiting for a message and to go on ahead."

"He's been looking forward to this for months," the other guy said. "Ice algae blooms are so incredibly cool."

An SUV started honking as the driver inched forward. They moved aside as the car pulled over. The driver hopped out and began to unload leather duffels and suitcases.

"Hermès and vintage Vuitton," Jonah said. "That is definitely not the luggage of a scientist."

A man stepped out dressed in faded jeans and a parka. He wore sunglasses, a baseball cap, and sneakers. He was speaking into a phone. "Don't forget my bottled water!" he barked at the driver.

"Bingo," Jonah said. "Hollywood. My people."

The man leaned down to help a woman out of the car. She was tiny and seemed to be fashioned out of sinew and air. She was dressed all in black, and large sunglasses concealed much of her face, giving her the look of a giant insect.

"Janelle Beladon," Jonah said. "The most elegant woman in the world."

"This jet lag is freakin' killing me," they heard her say.

A shower of flashbulbs went off as the movie star headed toward the gangway. A tall, silver-haired man greeted her warmly. He was wearing a white captain's hat with a gold anchor emblazoned on the front.

"Peter Zimmer," Jonah murmured. "Our host."

Crew members swarmed over the luggage, tagging and organizing it onto trolleys.

The man who had been riding in the car with

Janelle Beladon caught sight of Jonah. He waved his phone. "Jonah Wizard!" He strode toward him. "This is ultimate good karma, brother! Love it! I am your biggest fan of all time! I've been calling your agent for weeks!" He held out a hand. "Lloyd Trueman."

"How's it shaking, bro?" Jonah asked, immediately switching into his fake overdone hip-hop drawl. He bumped Lloyd's fist instead of shaking his hand.

"Are you on the *Titanic II*? Love it! I can pitch you on a film idea—Janelle's next picture—and she needs a sidekick to bring in the teens. Action movie—a ship gets hijacked in Tierra del Fuego and then gets sucked into a vortex that's a portal, get it? We open in another world, only it's in two dimensions, and one is brain waves! It's like Flat Stanley meets the X-Men. Genius, am I right?"

"Sounds crazy, bro," Jonah said.

"Totes! In a good way. Plus it's got a great message about humanity, you know? Janelle is very into that spiritual whole-earth thing. It's a deep story, same guy that did *Explosive Action*. You'd be perfect for the sidekick. The kid with the troubled past."

"We've only got one problem," Jonah said. "I'm not on the ship. It's full. I just flew down to see if there were any cancellations."

"Let me work my connections. I'm buds with Pete. In the meantime, come and have a snack in my suite, meet Janelle. I've got kale chips!"

"Can I bring my posse?"

"It's all good!"

"Flat Stanley meets the X-Men?" Dan murmured.

"You see what I have to deal with in order to live large like I do?" Jonah muttered through his smile.

Lloyd greeted Peter Zimmer, who had just finished welcoming a couple with air kisses.

"Pete, my man! Love the hat!"

Peter Zimmer touched the brim of his captain's hat. "Thanks. It would be corny, but I'm wearing it ironically." It was clear that Lloyd's "bud" Peter had no clue who Lloyd was. "Welcome aboard! The purser will want to see your tickets just ahead."

"No problem!" Lloyd said. "Looking forward to good times. Icebergs, gotta love it! Can you do me a favor and rustle up an extra cabin? This is my homey, Jonah Wizard. He and Janelle go way back."

It never failed to amaze Cara how rich and famous people were drawn to each other like moths on a lightbulb. Peter completely ignored the group and turned to Jonah. He bumped his fist in a casual way, as though they'd been friends forever. "So good to see you," he said. "I'm a fan. You know I'd love to accommodate you, but we are fully booked. I'll get in touch with my ticket agent and we'll set you up in a suite for a cruise of your choosing next fall."

"Sounds good," Jonah said.

Well, that took care of that. No cabin for Jonah. It wasn't going to be that easy. But Cara hadn't expected it to be.

"Got my friends here for a quick send-off in my suite," Lloyd said. "That cool?"

"That's fine. Just check in with the purser; we'll need their names. Doberman! These guests can come aboard with Mr. Wizard," Zimmer said to a tall man in a navy suit. "You only have about fifteen minutes," he warned Lloyd.

Doberman stepped forward, a tall, trim officer who looked resplendent in his navy uniform and cap. "Name, young man?"

"John Paul Jones," Dan blurted. "These are my sisters, Martha and Abigail."

"Chadwick Templeton," Ian said.

"My posse from Hollywood," Jonah said quickly. He put a hand on Hamilton. "And this is H—Sam Holter, my bodyguard."

Doberman entered their names. "Enjoy your visit. The all ashore announcement will be in exactly fourteen minutes."

Jonah engaged Lloyd in conversation about *Explosive Action*, and the rest of the gang slipped away.

Mission accomplished. For now.

"Chadwick Templeton?" Cara asked Ian. "That's the fakest fake alias I've ever heard."

"I went to boarding school with Chadwick," Ian said. "Nasty guy. Cheated at tennis."

They prowled the hallways, trying to look legitimate yet scope out a place to stow away. No more jokes, no more teasing. They moved fast and purposefully, their gazes noting every closet, every common room. There just didn't seem to be anywhere to hide. They walked through lounges with picture windows and soft sofas and beautiful lamps, through a large, paneled dining room and a book-lined library, even a small theater. The staff was everywhere, briskly walking through the rooms, checking to make sure everything was perfect.

"We can't get belowdecks," Hamilton said after they passed a door marked CREW ONLY. "It's locked-card access."

The announcement "All ashore who's going ashore" came over the PA system.

Jonah texted Ian. Cara looked over Ian's shoulder.

GOTTA BREEZE BRO. FOUND A CRANNY YET?

NOT YET, Ian replied.

TOLD MY MAN LLOYD YOU ALL ALREADY
LEFT. HE'LL CHECK YOU OUT WITH THE
PURSER. SO BETTER FIND A PLACE TO STOW
OR GO ASHORE. THEY'RE CHECKING TICKETS
EVERYWHERE. SEE U.

Cara nudged Ian. A ship's officer headed down the hallway, checking tickets. They turned and went the opposite way. Ahead of them were the same two young scientists they'd seen on the pier. Cara slowed her steps so that they could eavesdrop.

"Yeah, Hardcastle never showed up. Weird."

"Oh, man. Jumped ship, huh. Tagamayer's going to bust a gut."

"Because Rollo handled the PowerPoint, am I right?"

"Word. Didn't he have the cabin right next to yours?"

"Yeah. At least I won't have to listen to Iron Maiden in the mornings."

"An empty cabin," Amy whispered.

Without having to confer, they all spread out, keeping the two young scientists in view. One opened one door, the other the door opposite, and they both walked in. The doors banged shut.

Ian and Amy were slightly ahead. They hesitated outside the door to the empty cabin.

A ship's officer turned the corner. "Can't master the key card?" He smiled.

Ian held up a credit card, concealing most of it. "I keep trying, but . . . These kind folks were trying to assist me."

"He thinks it needs a slot!" Amy said. "I tried to tell him it's a sensor!" She reached out to grab the card, and Ian dropped it. Ham speeded up suddenly and walked by, kicking the card under the door as if by accident.

"Oops," he said. "Sorry, dude." He walked off, whistling.

The officer winced. "I wish he wouldn't do that," he said. "Crew members are a superstitious lot. We think that whistling calls up storms. Never whistle on a boat, young man. Bad enough that we're on a ship named *Titanic*," he muttered.

"Wouldn't dream of whistling, no sir," Ian promised. "But now I've lost my key card!"

"I can help you," the officer said. "Your name, sir?"

"Rollo Hardcastle."

The officer consulted his tablet. "Yes, Mr. Hardcastle. With the scientific group."

Ian ran a hand through his hair, mussing it. "Graduate student in geothermal energy. I know tons about volcanoes, but not much about key card sensors, I'm afraid."

Ian was perfect, Cara thought admiringly. He'd transformed himself from a privileged Brit into an addled egghead.

"Yes. Well, this is a maiden voyage. Bound to be a few mishaps here and there."

The officer took his pass card and held it briefly against the sensor. The door swung open.

"Keep your hands on that card, Mr. Hardcastle. You'll need it to charge purchases and also to sign in and out when we go ashore in Antarctica."

"Absolutely," Ian promised.

As soon as he was out of sight, the others turned back and crowded into the tiny cabin.

Ian turned to Cara. "You have to get off the ship," he said. "You've got to stay in Ushuaia."

"Why me?" Cara felt her cheeks go red.

"Ian is right," Amy said. "The Internet connection is going to get spotty. We've got to have a digital coordinator, and that's you. You must keep in contact with Nellie and Sammy and any Cahills who aren't in the Outcast camp. And if anything happens . . . if we fail . . ."

"Failure is not an option!" Ham reminded her.

". . . you've got to tell them what happened," Amy finished.

Cara felt stricken. Amy and Ian both looked so resolute. They were prepared for anything, she realized. Even not coming back.

"But . . ." she started. She tried to find an argument. She didn't want to leave them. She wanted to say, *You're my family now.*

Aren't you?

"It's an order, Cara," Ian said.

"I don't take orders," she snapped.

Amy shot Ian an exasperated glance. She touched Cara's arm. "We need you to do this. We have to use your skills in the best way possible."

It did make sense. She saw that. But why did she feel . . . abandoned? "I don't want to!"

Ian nodded. "I know. Jonah doesn't, either. But he knows he's too visible. Better to have two of you ashore. You can help us more there. Cara, you're the one holding the network together." His dark gaze was serious. "Each one of us has a job to do."

Cara's anger drained away. She swallowed against the lump in her throat. "I won't you let down."

"You never do," Ian said.

CHAPTER 27

Singapore

That evening at the Chens', Nellie unwrapped the weapon from her scarf and studied it. It was a steel spear about a foot long, with a menacingly sharp blade on each end. In the center was a rotating ring.

"I've never seen anything like this before," she said. "What is it?" She held it up.

"No idea," Sammy said. "I just know it was almost in your head." He put his arms around her. "Will you lose all respect for me when I tell you I was scared?"

"I was scared, too. You almost got yourself killed trying to tackle him."

"I wanted to kill him."

Nellie rested her head against his shoulder. "He would have killed *you*."

"At that moment, I didn't care."

Nellie drew back. "Sammy, he knew my name."

"I know. I don't like this."

"Did you notice that he called us *kiddos*? That's what I call Amy and Dan."

"Coincidence?"

"No." Nellie shook her head. "It was a threat, I'm sure of it. Remember how he emphasized it? He wanted me to know that the inner circle was invaded. There're only a few people who know I call Amy and Dan *kiddos*. And I trust all of them."

She looked at him worriedly. "It was a threat just as much as the spear was." She carefully wrapped her scarf around it. "The first thing we have to do is figure out what exactly this is."

Sammy suddenly crossed to the window. He motioned to Nellie to switch off the light.

"What is it?" she whispered.

"Somebody's out there."

Nellie moved through the dusky room and peered out behind the curtain. The trees and shrubbery she'd admired now seemed treacherous, places for people to hide.

A shadow moved out from the wall. Nellie tensed.

But it was only Mabel, a blur of white shirt against dark green.

Sammy let out a relieved breath and pushed open the French doors. They walked out onto the patio.

"Mabel!" Nellie exclaimed. "You scared us. What are you doing out here?"

"Shhh," she said, drawing them farther into the shadows. "I have to talk to you! Before you go inside. I found something out while you were gone." Mabel looked around. "I think . . . I think my parents might be in league with the Outcast."

"What makes you say that?" Sammy shot an uneasy glance at Nellie. "I can't believe it."

Mabel's face grew stormy. "Right. I imagine things. I'm too sensitive. I read too much. I need to calm down and go to my room. I've heard it all, Sammy, but I didn't expect to hear it from you!"

Sammy took a breath. "Okay. I'm sorry. What did you find out?"

"I did some investigating on the home computer," Mabel said. "My mom's password is so lame—the first two letters of all her kids' names. I was just nosing around, and, Sammy, there was a file with your father's name on it!"

"That makes sense. Our fathers have been friends forever."

"No, it's a work file! From his lab! My dad is in finance. He wouldn't understand a bunch of science stuff."

"Okay. I know my father is looking for investors to seed his new company. He probably sent it to your dad."

"But I tracked back in the downloads. It wasn't him who sent it! Patricia Oh forwarded it!"

"Patricia Oh!" Nellie exchanged a glance with Sammy.

"I'm guessing that she's not friends with your dad," Mabel said. "It was all these lab notes from some experiments he did on algae fermentation and combustion rates. . . ."

"For his biofuel research, yes," Sammy said. "He's been trying to perfect it for years. He's written papers that have been published. It's not a secret."

"But this seemed really secret!"

"And why would Patricia Oh forward it to Mabel's dad?" Nellie asked.

"It doesn't make sense," Sammy admitted.

"It makes sense if it was *stolen*," Mabel said triumphantly.

"There could be another explanation," Nellie said. But she couldn't think of one. These were Sammy's godparents. Would James betray his best friend?

Suddenly, she remembered meeting him this morning. She'd called Amy and Dan her *kiddos*. Suspicion sent a jolt through her.

"Well, I'm going to find out," Mabel declared.

"You'd spy on your own parents?" Nellie asked.

"Sure! I do it all the time!" Mabel said. "I mean, usually it's about vacation plans or Christmas presents. It's never anything huge like this. It's just that . . . I have to know things. I don't like being kept in the dark."

"Mabel, I don't want you to spy on your parents," Sammy said. "That's just wrong, no matter what. And anyway, there's an easy way to solve this mystery. I'll just ask my dad about it. He'll clear it up."

But Sammy looked uneasy. Nellie knew he was worried because he hadn't heard from his parents.

"Okay, call him right now," Mabel said. "It's morning in San Francisco."

Reluctantly, Sammy dug for his phone. He punched out the number on speed dial. He pressed the phone to his ear. Nellie saw his face change.

"The number's been disconnected," he said.

"Something weird is going on," Mabel said. "I told you!"

"Mabel, this isn't a game," Sammy said. "This is serious. More serious than you know. I can't let you—"

Mabel's voice rose in fury. "You can't stop me!"

"Stop you from what?"

James Chen loomed out of the shadows. He put his hand on his daughter's shoulder and gave her a tight smile. "What mischief are you planning?"

Nellie stared at that hand on Mabel's shoulder. It seemed heavy, threatening. And the smile was too wide. She felt suddenly afraid.

"I'm going to destroy him in tennis tomorrow," Mabel said.

"We don't use that tone with guests, though, do we, petal. And I don't think Sammy is in the mood for tennis. Come inside, everyone. It's time for dinner. Tiff has been worried. She didn't know where you were," he said to Nellie and Sammy. It sounded like an accusation.

"Sightseeing," Nellie said, keeping her voice light. "Sammy wanted to show me some of his old haunts."

"Ah. Good."

Tiff stood in the lighted doorway. Her anxious face broke into a smile. "I didn't realize you'd returned. Thank goodness you're back! Mabel, go wash your hands. No arguments, go!"

With a despairing look at them, Mabel dashed back into the house.

Nellie wondered what to do. The Chens looked so concerned. Even if Mabel was right—and she was hoping against hope that she wasn't—it wouldn't do any harm to tell the Chens what had happened to them in the park. She wanted to watch their faces.

"We ran into some trouble," Nellie admitted. Sammy gave her a quick, startled glance, and she gave him an imperceptible nod that meant *Go with me on this.* She fished in her bag and carefully withdrew the weapon. She held it up in the light. She knew they would be looking at the spear. She was looking at them.

"Somebody threw this at us. It could have been a random mugging, but we don't know. Do you know what it is?"

Nellie caught a lightning-flash look from husband to wife. *They know.*

"I have no idea," James said. "But this is alarming."

"From now on, you must take our car and driver wherever you go," Tiff said in a concerned tone.

Yes, so you can keep tabs on us.

"You are incredibly generous," Nellie said. And she smiled at her lovely hosts.

CHAPTER 28

Cape Horn, Drake Passage

"Dan?" Amy stared at the ceiling. "Am I still alive?"

"Yes, Amy."

"Oh. Too bad."

Ham grunted. He was curled up on the floor on a mountain of pillows. Ian had commandeered the couch because it was closest to the bathroom.

The ship rolled, hesitated, and plunged.

"It's kind of fun," Dan said. "Think of it as a rodeo."

"Stop," Amy pleaded through gritted teeth. "Your words are hurting my face."

The sea had been calm as they'd motored out of Beagle Channel and into the ocean. Once they'd hit Drake Passage, the swells had increased to twenty, then thirty feet. They'd hit one of the sudden storms the passage was famous for. Steady, cold rain fell, mixed with peppering hail. The crew had put up rope handrails on the decks and tucked barf bags in the passageway railings, but nobody ventured out. Most people were staying in their cabins.

Amy, Ham, and Ian had fallen so sick and dizzy that they were unable to move. They all wore wristbands for seasickness, but nothing could withstand the assault of the swells outside their window.

Dan, however, felt close to normal. Hungry—but that was normal.

"Okay, guys, I'm maxing out on the moaning," Dan said. He switched on the closed-circuit TV, which ran a schedule of activities. "There's a seal lecture up in the lounge and they're serving cookies and hot chocolate."

Ian stood, lurched, and ran to the bathroom.

"Don't. Mention. Food." Hamilton grunted each word.

"My point is that most people will be in their cabins or at the lecture, so I can explore."

With her eyes closed, Amy said, "See if you can steal a pass key."

"Right. Anybody want cookies?"

"Dude, leave immediately or I will kill you," Ham said.

Ian started out of the bathroom.

"Okay, Onions," Dan said, and Ian bolted back inside the bathroom again.

Dan left, quietly shutting the door. Walking was easy if you just expected the floor to heave and you didn't mind slamming into walls. Using handhold after handhold, he lurched down the passageway.

They had only thirty-six hours before disaster struck. Dan figured that the first place he should nose around should be the places passengers weren't allowed. He hesitated by a door marked CREW ONLY, but he knew he couldn't get in without a magnetic card. He'd have to steal one. The crew would be in the common spaces, so he headed through the interior passage, following the signs to DINING SALOON and LIBRARY and LOUNGE as well as a small restaurant called CAFÉ PARISIEN. It was modeled after the restaurant on the *Titanic*. Dan pressed his nose against the glass and tried to imagine women in gowns and men in white ties, drinking champagne. Not knowing that the iceberg was waiting out in the North Atlantic, thinking they were safe on an unsinkable ship.

Just like all the people in their luxurious cabins on the *Titanic II*.

Outside the portholes he could see nothing but endless, churning gray sea that met endless, opaque gray sky. Not an iceberg to be seen.

"Are you looking for the lounge, young man?" A crew member materialized out of a side passage. "There's an excellent lecture beginning in five minutes."

"Uh, yes," Dan said. He studied the crewman. There was a cord around his neck, and the end disappeared into a pocket in his jacket. That's where the card was. The ship suddenly rolled, and Dan was thrown up against the guy. He planted his hands on his chest and fumbled with an alligator clip. His fingers slid along the plastic . . .

"Oops, there you go." The crew member pushed him carefully to his feet. "You'll get the hang of it. This way, sir."

Dan had no choice but to follow. He had just missed lifting the card.

The lounge was all mahogany and brass, with inviting deep seats, gleaming wood tables, and flat screens hanging from the ceiling so that there wasn't a bad vantage point in the place. There was something that could be a Picasso hanging over the sofa. Maybe it was a Picasso. Basically, it all looked like a fancy hotel lobby, if you didn't notice that everything was bolted down.

Only two people sat in the lounge, one of them wearing a Cubs T-shirt and the other hanging on to a table with both hands. Outside the picture windows, waves towered as the ship plunged its way through them.

A steward in a white jacket approached. "May I get you something from the buffet, sir?"

The boat plunged into a wave that seemed to suck it down to the center of the earth. Dan felt his stomach rise into his throat. He sat down quickly. The boat shuddered, then climbed the wave, seeming to balance on top for long seconds before plunging down again. The passenger who had been holding the table suddenly bolted toward the bathroom.

"Um, no thanks," Dan said. "I think I'll just sit."

The man in the Cubs T-shirt spoke. He jerked his chin toward the door. "That was our lecturer, Dr. Gilman. Looks like it's just you and me." He looked like a genial guy in tortoiseshell glasses, his silver hair cut short. "The trick is to keep your eye on the horizon."

"Yeah," Dan said. "If only it didn't keep disappearing."

"Ha! Exactly! Well, too bad about Dr. Gilman. I was looking forward to the talk. Leopard seals are the most vicious predators in Antarctica. Can rip a penguin out of its bones. More fun than krill. That's my specialty." He stuck out his hand. "Dr. Jeff Tagamayer."

Dan shook his hand. "J. P. Jones here. What's a krill?"

The man's face lit up. "Do you want to hear my lecture?"

"Antarctica is the coldest, driest, windiest continent," Dan told the others when he returned. "It's the only continent without an indigenous human population. That means no humans ever lived there! Plus, all the countries got together in 1959 and made this treaty that there could be no military bases, only scientific ones. Dr. Jeff told me that scientists work on all kinds of cool stuff in Antarctica. Not just penguins and seals and whales, but global warming—did you know that the retreat of ice in western Antarctica means that the collapse of the entire ice sheet is *unstoppable* now? Icebergs are calving at an incredible rate—that means that major chunks are breaking off. They melt from below the sea and the cracks radiate up. Because of the massive melt of the ice, sea levels are going to rise by at least a meter all over the *planet*, maybe close to five meters, in only a couple of hundred years. Millions of people will be displaced! No more beach-front property! Miami will be underwater, people! Jeff says it's a huge problem. His specialty is phyto-plankton and krill, which are tiny but actually crustaceans. *Euphausia superba!* They feed on algae and plankton. Krill are teeny tiny, but are a main food source for a bunch of species, even blue whales if you can believe it, and the warmer water means the krill are migrating to different places, and that's endangering seals and penguins. It's already shrunk their habitats. They're migrating, and soon they'll run out of land. Did you know there are twenty-one species of penguins in Antarctica? Hey, speaking of penguins, did you know that fathers chew their food and then spit it into the baby penguins' mouths?"

Ian put a hand to his mouth and staggered for the bathroom yet again.

"Not only that, but there are scientists who are drilling down for hundreds of feet and discovering things about climate from about eight hundred thousand years ago! It has so much to teach us."

"Can it teach us to stop the boat from moving?" Ham asked, his eyes closed.

Amy rose on her elbows, one hand holding a damp washcloth to her forehead. "We're not here as tourists, Dan. We have to find out more about the *ship*."

"I know! I'm doing that, too! Dr. Jeff told me all this stuff while we toured the ship. He knows a huge amount about it. The ship is way past state-of-the-art; it's on to a whole new level of biotechnology."

"Dan." Amy pressed her fingers against her eyes. "Have you located any suspects? Anything suspicious?"

"Well, that's sort of impossible, because everyone is seasick. And my attempt to steal a key card was a bust. We need more activity on the ship for cover. But here's the good news—we're through Drake Passage. Jeff said the sea will get way calmer once we cross this imaginary line and we're in Antarctic waters. That means you can get up and get to work."

Ian staggered out of the bathroom. "Has anyone heard from Cara?"

"Still no reception, but Dr. Jeff says—"

Ian groaned from his position on the couch. "Can you go away now? I'd lift my head, but I think I would rather die."

"See you," Dan said.

Dan headed out the door and into the passageway. Maybe the ship was starting to stabilize already. He didn't feel as though he was walking on a bouncy castle quite as much.

Dan rounded the corner. Ahead was the ship's officer who had checked them in on board. Doberman. If he recognized Dan, he'd remember that he'd only been cleared to visit Lloyd Trueman's cabin.

Dan immediately lurched to the side and turned his head, hoping Doberman would just pass by.

No luck. "Can I help you, young man? Are you ill?"

"Just a little bit," Dan mumbled. "I'm okay."

"Let me help you to your cabin."

"No! I feel okay. Really."

Doberman looked at him closer. "Are you with the high school group? They're all the way at the other end of the ship."

"Right. I guess I got lost."

Doberman continued to regard him. Dan could see the flare of suspicion in his eyes. He hadn't placed him yet, but any moment he would. "May I see your key card, young man? I can direct you."

"Sure." Dan patted his pockets. "Gosh, I thought I had it . . ."

"Passengers are requested to wear it, sir. It does come with a chain necklace."

"Yeah, but it didn't match my outfit."

"Do you have your ID on you?"

"Ah . . . no. Must be with my key card!"

Doberman whipped out his tablet. "Why don't you tell me your name, and I can look you up on the manifest. Then we can issue you a new card."

"I'm sure it's in my room . . ." Desperately, Dan pretended to search his pants.

Then, down the passageway, Dr. Jeff turned the corner and headed toward them.

Dan froze. Dr. Jeff knew him as J. P. Jones, an imaginary person who was definitely not on the manifest. He was trapped.

"Well, hello!" Dr. Jeff said cheerfully.

"You know this young man, Dr. Tagamayer?"

Dr. Jeff hesitated. Dan pleaded him with his eyes, but he didn't know what he was asking for.

Dr. Jeff put his hand on Dan's shoulder. "Of course I do! This is my research assistant, Rollo Hardcastle. We were just heading to the lounge. He's going to help me fix my PowerPoint for tonight. Speaking of which, we'd better hurry!"

Surprise propelled Dan down the hall, out of earshot of Doberman.

"Thanks for the save," Dan said. "But why?"

"Why not?" Jeff asked him, his eyes twinkling. "It isn't every day I get to meet a legend. Dan Cahill, I presume?"

CHAPTER 29

Singapore

Sammy lay awake at three A.M. The house had been quiet for hours. The Chens' chef had prepared a sumptuous meal with many courses, but conversation had been strained. Portions of his favorite foods were heaped on his plate, but the food stuck in his throat.

How could this warm, smiling couple, people he'd known his whole life, be *bad*? He couldn't believe his godparents could betray the Cahills with that maniac Outcast.

He kept checking his phone, but his parents didn't respond to any messages he'd left on the home or office phones. That worry was a buzz at the back of his brain. They didn't check in with him constantly, but they always told him when they went away.

Over and over he tried to remember the past, tried to think of an indication that the Chens were power hungry. All he could remember were masses of flowers in Tiff's arms as she filled vases, wonderful trips to gardens and museums, and the gift of cooking lessons on his sixteenth birthday. Thoughtful godparents, beautiful hosts. This house had been a dream of luxury and consideration.

But had there been things he hadn't seen? Strain on the corner of James's mouth. Tiff's need to control. He remembered going swimming once before breakfast, how she'd come out with a tight smile and a towel. *We swim in the afternoons, Sammy. Breakfast is at seven.*

And hadn't his father hinted that he and James had had a falling-out? Sammy had forgotten. He remembered his father turning away, a shrug, an evasive wave of his hand. *We're not as close as we used to be. People change.*

And what had always been missing in this house? Spontaneous laughter. Snacks in the kitchen. Staying up past bedtime. No, the house was run a certain way, and you got the hang of it fast. And it was all so pleasant, so luxurious, you didn't mind.

Was this house *too* perfect? Was the thing that was missing summed up in one word, like *fun*? Or *love*?

He flipped over again.

There was more to learn here. But how to find it?

There could be reasons that his father sent his lab notes to James, couldn't there? But James wasn't a scientist. He wouldn't be able to decipher those notes. Algae was surprisingly complicated. Sometimes he had had trouble following his father's explanations about biofuels and hazards. . . .

Sammy sat up. Wait a second. Had Mabel said *combustion?*

Sammy threw back the light coverlet. He pulled on his jeans and tiptoed out into the common area. He opened Nellie's door and crept inside. She was sleeping deeply, one arm flung out into the path of moonlight that striped her bed.

He leaned closer. "Nellie," he whispered.

The next thing he knew, a fist had rammed into his throat and he was on his back on the floor, seeing stars.

"Haven't we been here before?" he croaked. "I seem to remember you once hit me with a fire extinguisher."

"It was an accident!" Nellie hopped up, wringing her hands. "Sammy, you have to stop *surprising* me! Are you okay?"

"I . . . think . . . so," he said.

"Here, let me help you. Sit on the bed. Take a deep breath. It's a good thing I was half-asleep or I *really* would have clocked you."

He looked at her, wide-eyed. "That one will do."

"What's the matter? Why did you come in?" Nellie tucked her legs underneath her and leaned toward him.

"Biofuels," he said.

"Oh, good. Because that's exactly what I want to talk about at three A.M."

"It was something Mabel said. *Combustion.*"

"Right. Meaning something could blow up. Like algae can blow up? I didn't get that."

"No. Not like algae. Like biofuel. That's powering a ship. That's my dad's big secret project."

Nellie's eyes went wide. She swallowed hard. "Talk."

Sammy sat cross-legged across from her. "This isn't my field, but I've talked enough to my dad to get a lot of it. There are a number of practical problems deriving fuel from algae. If it could be perfected, it could be awesome, because the development could be carbon-neutral."

"Meaning it won't take huge amounts of energy to make energy."

"Exactly. Lots of scientists and companies are working on this. It was my dad who found this new species of algae . . . he called it *Pediastrum mayanum* after my mom."

"Aw. Sweet!"

"It had all these properties that my dad saw could solve lots of problems that other kinds of algae had in terms of processing them into fuel. There was only one problem. It's extremely unstable, with a high combustion rate."

"You mean algae *can* blow up?"

"Well, not in its natural state, but when it's being processed. Because you need massive amounts of it, right? It just needs a stabilizing agent—an X factor, if you will. Not as easy as it sounds. Then my dad reads this paper on ice algae, and boom, something clicked. Science is so *amazing* that way! You find stuff in other fields and all of a sudden, connections start firing! Then you're off on a new direction, and solving way more problems than you thought—"

"Sammy, you are the most adorable nerd, but can you stick to the point?"

"Right. Something about ice algae was the key, some sort of stabilizing structure. . . ." Sammy clutched his hair, something he did when he couldn't remember a detail. "I don't remember! But my dad's brain just starts going in a new direction. He goes to see the scientist and asks to study his research. It looks promising, so they do some experiments together in this guy's lab."

"Did they discover the X factor?"

"No, just other cool stuff."

Nellie slumped back, disappointed. "Oh."

"But here's the thing. The last time we talked about it, he was super excited. He said he went back over the notes, and they'd missed something. He felt pretty close. He was going to go back to this guy, back to the lab."

"But when was that?"

"Couple of months ago, maybe. It's funny, he stopped talking about it and I forgot to follow up. I was busy with my graduate project."

"So maybe he did it! Maybe he found the X factor, or he thought he did, and he was waiting to tell you!

Sammy, the *Titanic II* is running on biofuel. Some sort of incredible new green technology! What if there's a connection here?"

"I know, that's what I was thinking. But I can't see how it could happen, really. My dad could have solved the X factor, but still, it would have been *years* away from being perfected."

"Don't scientists ever have a sudden breakthrough that zooms them ahead? Isn't that what you just said before?"

"Sure, all the time, but in this case the fuel would have to be manufactured. There'd have to be a factory and everything. . . ."

"Oh, like you've never been in a secret factory."

Sammy sat up straighter. "Good point."

Nellie's fingers drummed on the coverlet. "We have to get a look at that file. It's on the Chens' computer. Do you know all the names of the kids?"

"David, Howard, William, and Mabel."

"*DaHoWiMa.*" Nellie swung her feet off the bed. "Come on. It's time to do a little breaking and entering."

CHAPTER 30

Titanic II, *Antarctica*

"Wake up, Amy." The voice invaded her dreams.

"Go away. I'm sick."

"No. You're not." It was Ian. "We're in Antarctic waters. The ship isn't lurching about like Ham attempting to dance."

"Hey, dude. I heard that."

Amy opened her eyes. The curtains were open. An iceberg sailed by. Or was it a mirage?

No, she corrected. They had sailed by an iceberg.

Ian smiled. "Welcome to Antarctica."

Amy stumbled to the window. She could see the horizon instead of a wall of water. Outside, a silvery blue sky arced over a deep blue sea. Icebergs dotted the seascape, one as tall as a building, and others scored with undulations created by wind and waves. One was a shimmering portal, an arch through which Amy saw her first penguin as it slid across an icy floe and splashed into the sea.

Inside the ice were hidden colors: shades of blue she hadn't known existed, electric aquamarine, the palest powdery blue, the sheerest green. A huge bird flew by, its white wings beating rhythmically. Its wingspan must have been close to ten feet.

"Albatross," Ian said.

"Magic," she said.

They were silent a moment, all of them lined up at the window. On the other side was a world of astonishing beauty, so strange and new that it seemed unreal. *How lucky we are to see this*, Amy thought, remembering all that Dan had said about how endangered the environment was. Hard on the heels of that was, *We must save this ship.*

Ian rubbed his hands together. "Yes. Now that we've fully appreciated the beauties of this amazing continent, let's get going."

He was interrupted by the chime of a text. Ian checked his phone.

"It's from the Outcast."

HAVING A BLAST? IT'S NOW DAY FIVE.
LET'S SPEED UP THE TIMELINE. SET YOUR
CLOCKS. FOR 6 PM EXACTLY! THAT'S WHEN
THINGS GO BOOM!

Ian put down his phone, his face grim. "It's four o'clock now. That only gives us two hours!"

Just then Dan barreled through the door followed

by a shy-looking man with glasses. "Hey, everyone, meet Dr. Jeff. He's going to solve all our problems!"

"Well, I don't know about that." The man shrugged in a modest way. "But I'll do anything to help out Grace's grandchildren."

"Way to stay undercover," Ian said with an annoyed glance at Dan.

"No worries. I'm an Ekat," Dr. Tagamayer said cheerfully. "I wouldn't have blown Dan's cover, but he almost got caught by the purser. I've been in South Pole Station for a year. Totally out of the Cahill loop. So I don't know what you're doing here, but I want to help. My assistant got sick in Ushuaia, so one of you can be Rollo Hardcastle, and if anyone stops you, just tell them you're working with me. Cahills have to stick together."

"That's a concept that seems to have been mislaid lately," Ian murmured. But he stood and shook Dr. Jeff's hand. "Welcome to the family," he said. "We can use the help."

The gang split up, the better to fully explore the ship. Dr. Jeff had gone off to ask Peter Zimmer for a tour of the engine room. Ian felt the ticking of the clock with every beat of his heart. What was that American expression that Hamilton always used? *Crunch time.*

Now that he had a cover story, he felt a bit safer on

the ship. He would blend in. He'd donned a hideous fleece garment in order to pass as a student. Once they prevented the disaster and got off this ship, he would contemplate the American love of fleece and toss this one in the garbage.

Ian opened the door to the outside. A blast of wind almost knocked him down, and the cold hit him so hard his teeth hurt. Tears sprang to his eyes and ran down his face. Every exposed piece of skin was painful. Ian clapped his hands over his ears and bent over to protect himself from the agony. Suddenly, he *loved* fleece.

The door slammed behind him. He took a breath and felt his lungs expand. It was the sharpest, cleanest air he'd ever breathed. Iceberg formations loomed on either side of the ship, incredibly beautiful ledges and towers, some hundreds of feet high. An island sat in the distance, with snowy cliffs and black sand beaches. People were lined up, hanging on to the railings in the middle of the gusts, with binoculars pointed at the moving black dots on the beach. Ian realized that they were penguins. He stood for a moment, trying to trace their comical movements. When he turned and looked out to sea, a whale casually breached, its tail a lazy flourish as it sank back into the sea.

Ian wasn't much for nature—he much preferred a busy London street—but this was beyond spectacular. *Magic*, Amy had said, and she was right.

He hurried along the deck to the bridge. When he pushed open the door, he was glad to see a crowd of science nerd students crowded around the instruments. They'd help with camouflage.

Passengers were welcome on the bridge, and Ian stopped for a moment, pretending to study the rows of electronic instruments. At the other end of the bridge he saw some officers conferring. They were frowning and speaking in low voices. Ian skirted the map table and, pretending to admire a breaching whale, edged closer to see if he could overhear.

"Captain wants to keep on to Paradise Harbor," one of the officers said. "Too windy for landings on Deception Island, and there's snow coming. The passengers have had enough of rough seas. We can hit it on the way back if we have time."

"So we'll just do the staff transfer then?"

"Second Mate Anderson will ferry Dr. Tagamayer to the Deception Island station."

"Why's he leaving early? Can't wait to get back to civilization, huh?"

"Well, he didn't last very well on the winter expedition, did he? Heard they had to airlift him out last April."

"Sick?"

"No, just spooked. Too much dark, too much ice."

"Man, is *he* in the wrong profession."

They chuckled, and Ian moved away, his ears buzzing with what he'd heard.

Last *April*? That was almost a year ago. That meant Dr. Jeff had lied to them. He'd only lasted a month at the South Pole!

Maybe Dr. Jeff had been embarrassed to admit he had to be airlifted out.

But somehow Ian didn't think so.

It meant that he had been around for much of last year. Plenty of time to be recruited by the Outcast.

And he was leaving the ship shortly before it was scheduled to explode.

Ian texted the others.

```
JEFF TAGAMAYER BEING ESCORTED OFF SHIP
TO DECEPTION ISLAND. V SUSPICIOUS. LIED
ABOUT SPENDING WINTER AT POLE. I'LL GET
CARA TO INVESTIGATE. MEANWHILE LOCATE
HIM! COULD BE IN ZIMMER'S CABIN.
```

He slipped the phone back in his pocket and headed off the bridge. The blast of wind made him stagger. In front of him was a crew member, and Ian slowed his pace, not wanting to attract attention. He buried his chin in his fleece.

It was too cold to walk slowly. Ian risked a quicker pace, coming up behind the crew member, who opened a door to the main passageway and passed through. Ian followed, glad to feel the warmth of the ship.

The crew member headed for the stairway, whistling a tune.

Whistling.

Bad luck.

No crew member would whistle aboard a ship.

Ian studied the man's stride, the way he moved, keeping his chin slightly angled and away from the passengers as they walked by.

Something about him was familiar. Very familiar.

Nellie had filled him in on Fiske's identification of the mystery guy.

It was Alek Spasky.

CHAPTER 31

Singapore

Their bare feet made no sound on the polished floors. The air conditioning hummed as they tiptoed into Tiff's office.

Nellie used her phone to illuminate the dark room. She switched on the computer.

Sammy pecked out the password. *"DaHoWiMa.* I'm in!"

Nellie hung over his shoulder as he clicked on the search engine. "Remind me to wipe the search history after we're done."

Sammy quickly searched through the computer and clicked on the file. He leaned forward, reading it quickly.

"Mabel was right," he groaned. "It's not only the paper he wrote with the biologist—that's been published. But it's his private lab notes! And it was forwarded to Patricia Oh!"

Nellie leaned over his shoulder. She tried to read the report, but all she saw were equations. Her brain hurt. "Who's Rollo?" she asked, pointing to the screen.

"That must be the lab assistant. RH. See, down here? They sign off on each day's notes with their initials." Sammy scanned the notes. "It's true. My father had a major breakthrough. He found the X factor! It's an agent that neutralized the combustibility ratio of the algae. Together, they raised the oil pressure in the tank, but if he altered the molecular structure by the pH factor . . . hmmm. Fascinating."

Nellie stared at the initials at the bottom of the report, DM. If only Darsh Mourad could speak to them!

"There's something else," Sammy said. He glanced up at her. "It's embedded in the notes. It's a detailed what-if scenario if the stabilizing agent isn't added. The effect of combusting fuel tanks aboard a moving vessel. It's a question of probabilities—how to institute emergency procedures in the event of human error. My father is meticulous. If he felt the fuel was too dangerous, he would stop the research. What if . . ."

". . . someone wasn't so meticulous," Nellie said, "or was evil. And handed this scenario over to the Outcast."

"And why does James Chen have it?" Sammy shook his head. "I can't believe my godfather could do this."

"Sammy, we need to investigate the other guy." She pointed to the initials at the end of the lab report. "JET. Do you . . ."

Nellie stopped short. "Oh. Shut *up*."

"What? I didn't say anything."

"No—JET. Do you know who this guy is?"

"He's a professor at the University of Chicago. He shouldn't be too hard to find."

"Chicago! Wasn't that what Sinead said?" Nellie leaned in closer so that they were practically nose to nose. "She overheard Patricia Oh say that the jet took off from Chicago with the package. It was him!"

"What?"

"Not a jet . . . not a plane, a person. JET. That's who stole the report! The other scientist! Maybe your dad mentioned to James what he was working on, and they got to the other guy. Bribed him or something. Sammy, how hard would it be to sabotage the ship?"

"Not hard. But you'd have to know what you were doing. These are precise calibrations."

"But JET *does* know. And he could be aboard that ship!"

Sammy looked pale. "You're right."

"Can you figure out how to fix it? Is there something Amy and Dan and the others can do to reverse the combustion cycle? We have to figure this out fast. We have less than a day!"

Sammy nodded, his face intent. "Let's see, I'm guessing that saboteur must have recalibrated the stabilizer and cut the concentration—"

Nellie held up a hand. "Shhh. I hear something."

Footsteps. Coming down the hall.

Sammy shut down the computer. Nellie looked around frantically. She opened a door and peeked around it. It was a home gym. She and Sammy slipped inside and closed the door behind them.

They saw a light stream from under the door. Footsteps going to the desk. The creak of a chair.

Nellie's heart thrashed. To have come so close! The answer was right there, in the computer. All she knew was that something in that biofuel was going to trigger a chemical reaction, and the ship was going to blow.

And her kiddos were on it. Along with Ian and Hamilton, and at least a hundred others.

She put her lips to Sammy's ear. "We have to tell them," she whispered.

Sammy took out his phone. He started a text to Jonah.

TRAPPED.

CHENS COULD BE IN LEAGUE W/OUTCAST.

BIOFUEL TO BLOW UP SHIP.

THERE'S ONE CHANCE THAT COULD WORK.

Nellie watched as Sammy closed his eyes in concentration. If anyone could do it, her science genius beautiful nerd could do it.

Sammy's thumbs went crazy, dancing on the screen.

The chair creaked again.

Nellie shrank back. She kept her eyes on the door.

She knew she couldn't rush genius. So she kept the words unspoken.

Hurry, Sammy. Hurry!

CHAPTER 32

Ushuaia, Argentina

Jonah checked his phone. Nothing.

"That's the third time in three minutes you've checked your phone," Cara said.

"Not a fan of downtime," Jonah said. He stretched out his arms over the seat back of the couch. They'd been sitting there for most of the day, waiting for something to happen.

He needed news or he'd go crazy. He'd heard that everyone was seasick except for Dan. He'd been filled in on Dan's enthusiasm for leopard seals and iceberg calving and emperor penguins. But he hadn't heard anything in over an hour. Internet connections could be wonky, he knew that, but his bro Ham was on that ship, and he felt like something was missing. Like his right arm. Cara was cool, but she couldn't replace the lug who had his back.

"Can't believe you can keep working on that thing."

"The digital world is full of trails people don't even know they're making," Cara said. "I might find something to help them. But there's nothing. That's the problem." Cara looked up. "That tailor who tried to drug Ian? No record of him. Zip. Berman ran the house, and he checked all records. Then I checked his checks and ran some deep background. Funicello was clear. Now those trails have disappeared."

"So, the guy wasn't who he said he was."

"Yeah. Figures. But what about Berman? All the records I checked before we hired him? Gone. He was an Ekat, worked in a resort in the Maldives. A concierge in Cannes, a butler in London. Impeccable references that I checked impeccably! And now? Gone. No digital trails. Benjamin Berman does not exist."

"Whoa."

"Yeah." Cara tossed the tablet aside and leaned her head back on the armchair. "I don't get fooled like this. It's unacceptable. I've tried and tried, and I can't figure it out."

"You okay?" Jonah asked. "'Cause you seem, well, clenched."

"Can't help myself," Cara said. "I'm worried that Ian will do something stupid. Like blow himself up."

"Ian's too smart to be stupid," Jonah said.

"He's an egomaniac. He takes too many chances. Thinks he's smarter than everybody else."

"Word. But that doesn't make him stupid," Jonah said. He thought a minute. "Usually."

"He doesn't know how to relate to ordinary people. He can be unbelievably dense. And condescending!"

"He's got some issues," Jonah agreed. "Got some faults, no question. He's a bro, though. Don't tell him I said that."

"I wish he wasn't such an idiot!"

Jonah gave the deep chuckle that *Film Today* magazine referred to as "maple syrup for the ears." "You and Ian have to work this out, because it's *painful* watching the two of you. You need to get honest and get together, if you don't mind my saying."

Cara lifted her chin. "I don't know what you mean."

"Right."

His phone buzzed in his hand.

"Anything?" Cara jumped up.

"Sammy."

She hurried to read the texts over his shoulder.

TRAPPED.

Jonah hunched over the phone. Waiting.

CHENS COULD BE IN LEAGUE W/OUTCAST.

BIOFUEL TO BLOW UP SHIP.

THERE'S ONE CHANCE THAT COULD WORK.

GOT IT. Jonah hit the keys, his stomach clenching.

SUSPECTS: ROLLO. ALSO A SCIENTIST J.E.T.

"Rollo," Jonah said to Cara. "That's the guy next door with the Do Not Disturb sign, right? The one who missed the boat?"

COMBUSTIBILITY BUILDUP AS OXYGEN ENTERS TANK. AS FUEL DECREASES O2 INCREASES. BUILDS UP PRESSURE. CHAIN REACTION POSSIBLE.

"Ask him what they can do!" Cara sputtered, but Jonah's fingers were already tapping out the same question.

THINKING.

"Think faster," Jonah murmured.

NOISES IN THE HOUSE

OVER AND OUT FOR NOW

They waited.
And waited.
Jonah exchanged a glance with Cara. Friends on a ship rigged to explode, friends trapped in an enemy's

house. And he was sitting here miles away, with no way to get to them. He had to do something!

Cara's fingers flew on her tablet. "I'm forwarding the texts to Ian."

She looked up, her face pale. "He says that the Outcast has given them a time limit. The ship is going to blow at six P.M.!"

Jonah slammed his hand down on the desk. "We've got to do something! Rollo!" Jonah suddenly bolted from the desk. "He'll have some answers."

He'd heard the maid tapping at the guy's door, asking if he wanted service. No answer for a day. Jonah knocked on the door, but there was no answer, not even a "Go away."

"Rollo, it's Jonah Wizard, bro. Time to join the living! No more of this Do Not Disturb. I am disturbing you!"

No answer.

"I'm going in," Jonah said.

The doors used old-fashioned keys. Cara lifted a bobby pin from her ponytail. "Try this."

Jonah inserted the pin and wiggled it. No luck. "It always works in the movies. Back up."

"No, Jonah! Wait!"

Too late. Jonah collided with the door shoulder-first, and bounced off.

Cara leaned over him. "Life doesn't come with stunt doubles, bro."

Jonah grabbed his shoulder. "Ow."

"What I was about to say was, our balconies are right next door to each other. We can climb over and see if the balcony door is open."

"Right. I knew that."

They hurried through their hotel room and onto the balcony. Jonah climbed over the railing and stepped across the distance onto the next balcony. He balanced, then pulled himself up and over. He tried the knob and it turned. He looked back at Cara.

"Stay there. I'll be right back."

"Are you kidding me? I'm coming." Cara executed the same maneuver and crowded in behind him.

The room was dark and stuffy. Jonah blinked, trying to adjust after the bright sunlight outside.

Then he saw a shape on the floor.

"Cara, wait outside."

"Would you stop treating me like a girl? I—" Cara stopped. "Oh. Oh!" She clutched Jonah's arm.

Jonah crossed to the body on the floor. He lay faceup, and Jonah knew immediately that Rollo was dead.

Death was so much different from the movies, Jonah thought. It hit you in a place that was deeper than you ever wanted to go.

Jonah stared down at the young man, who still wore an expression of surprise.

"We'll catch the guy who did it, bro," he said.

As he turned to go, his foot hit something. Jonah

crouched down to examine it. It was a metal spear, not long, but with an extremely sharp point. In the center of the spear was a small ring. As though someone could slip it over a finger to rotate it, fast, faster, until it was a blur of contained energy and velocity. And then they let it fly.

CHAPTER 33

Deception Island, Antarctica

Amy crouched by the Zodiac inflatable boats that were used for shore excursions. What was Dr. Jeff doing? It looked like he was taking a Zodiac by himself. That didn't make sense. Ian had said he was being escorted to the island.

Amy pressed herself back against the ship as Dr. Jeff looked around carefully, then threw a duffel into the Zodiac.

Dan and Ham emerged from the passageway, and she frantically signaled them to join her.

"He's taking off without an escort," Amy murmured.

"We went to Zimmer's cabin looking for him, but he never showed up," Dan said.

Dr. Jeff attached a hook to a Zodiac and lowered it down into the water. Then he clambered over the side onto the ladder. Amy heard the motor start a moment later.

She opened a nearby supply closet and slipped into a parka.

"What are you doing?" Dan asked.

She shoved her feet into boots. "Following him. He's got to be up to something. Come on."

Dan and Hamilton quickly grabbed parkas and boots. Ham lowered the Zodiac into the gray water and they climbed in. Dr. Jeff was already a speck heading toward the island. Amy started up the motor. She kept the speed low, tracking Dr. Jeff, who didn't look back.

"This is fun. I think my eyeballs are freezing," Hamilton remarked.

They skimmed through the ice floes, drawing closer and closer to the island. Out on the water, the wind was stronger, sending icy particles against their skin. Now Amy could see the cheerful penguins waddling on the beach and clustered in groups on ice floes. They looked so awkward and funny on land, but as they belly flopped on the ice and slid into the water, they turned into torpedoes of power and speed.

Amy wiped snow out of her eyes. She tried not to think of the ticking minutes, tried to focus on keeping Dr. Jeff's boat in sight. She felt in the pocket of the parka and found a wool hat. She pulled it on, down to her eyebrows. The Zodiac bumped along the water, sending freezing spray back at them as she zigzagged, keeping the cliffs and bergs between them and Dr. Jeff's boat.

"Deception Island is an old whaling center," Dan said over the noise of the engine. "The harbor is a caldera. You know, a collapsed volcano. Don't worry, the volcano hasn't erupted since the sixties. Destroyed the Chilean stations completely. And the British."

"That's encouraging," Ham said.

"Once we get past that point, we'll go through the narrows and be in a kind of horseshoe-shaped harbor."

The rocks loomed ahead in a palette of browns and blacks, now painted with the purest white snow. As the Zodiac rounded a rock formation the bay appeared, curled around the black volcanic sand. Amy slowed the engine and hugged the rocks as she turned into the narrows. Across the churning gray water, Dr. Jeff was beaching the boat.

He shouldered his duffel and walked up the shore. In a few minutes, he had disappeared through the whirling snow.

"He's probably headed up the beach toward the station," Dan guessed.

"Let's follow him." Amy steered toward the beach, keeping well away from Dr. Jeff's landing. They pulled the boat up on shore. The wind drove the wet snow against any exposed skin. It made it uncomfortable to walk, but at least the weather provided good cover.

Inquisitive penguins waddled toward them, their wings outstretched for balance.

"Chinstrap penguins," Dan noted. "See the line on their necks? Dr. Jeff told me about them while we explored the ship. He was a nice guy. I hate it when a good guy turns into a bad guy."

They raced up the beach. They could see Dr. Jeff's blue parka in the distance. There were no trees to hide behind, but ahead they saw abandoned buildings and old rusting tanks dotting the landscape, some six or seven stories tall.

"Whaling station," Dan said. "That's where they boiled the carcasses for oil. Look, you can still see whale bones on the beach."

"It's creepy," Amy said, thinking of the magnificent creatures she'd seen breaching off the ship. "It's like we're on Death Beach."

"Let's hope not," Dan muttered.

They moved from tank to tank, trying to keep Dr. Jeff in sight. It was soon clear that he was heading to the new structure, a bright blue station that was perched on metal stilts.

They walked closer, skirting an abandoned wooden building, the timbers sunk in sand. The skeleton of a whaling boat lay splintered nearby.

Amy stopped. There was just an expanse of sand between them and the station.

"If we keep going, he'll see us," she said. "Do you think there are people in the station?"

"There are only summer stations on this island," Dan said. "They could be gone. I heard the staff saying the scientists are starting to clear out for the winter."

"Doesn't look like there's any activity around," Hamilton said.

"Then what is he doing here?" Amy murmured.

"If we make a run for it, we can get underneath the station while he's opening that door," Hamilton suggested. "Once he's inside, he won't be able to see us. He's going up the stairs. We might make it."

As soon as he started up the stairs, they dashed toward the station. But when they were halfway across the snow, Jeff turned, as if he felt their presence.

"Okay, we blew it," Amy said, putting on a smile and waving. "Time to bluff our way out of this."

The three of them trudged toward the dwelling as Dr. Jeff headed down the stairs toward them.

"What are you doing here?" he asked. His welcoming smile was tight and annoyed.

"We didn't want to miss out on anything!" Amy answered, injecting a cheerful note in her voice. She was well aware of their isolation, of the fact that no one on the ship knew where they were. Still, she had Dan and Hamilton, and she felt confident that they could overpower Dr. Jeff if they had to. "We took a Zodiac out, and we saw you on the beach."

"You took a Zodiac out alone?" he asked, frowning. "And you couldn't have swiped out since you're stowaways. That could be dangerous. The weather is worsening. You took a big risk. You should go back to the ship right now. I'm just here to collect krill data. The crew has already left for the winter."

"We'd rather hang with you," Amy said. "Then we can go back together."

He looked displeased, but he hitched his bag higher on his shoulder and nodded. "I'm supposed to do the final close of the station. Come on."

He turned away, and Amy saw the stitched initials on his duffel.

JET

She remembered the text that Nellie had sent about Sinead. Not much to go on, Nellie had written. But this:

Sinead heard P Oh say that the jet has taken off from Chicago with the package.

Jeffrey E. Tagamayer. JET.

Her legs kept moving, following him up the metal staircase. She slipped her phone out of her pocket and tugged off one glove with her teeth. No reception.

Jeff opened the door and let them pass through. It slammed shut. The solid thud of the door sounded ominous.

They were in an open space divided into living and dining areas. A long table was pushed against a wall, the chairs upended over the table. Desks were over by a rolled-up rug. Bookshelves crammed with books and DVDs lined a wall, but there were no electronics. One corner held a bright purple sofa with multi-colored pillows.

"I didn't expect it to look so homey," Dan said. He was looking around with what seemed to be genuine interest, but Amy knew he was just as spooked as she was. The thing about Antarctica was that you felt you had been flung off the earth into some strange galaxy. Help seemed a million miles away. She sneaked a glance at her phone. They'd already spent an hour searching the ship and motoring here. One hour to go.

"Sure. The scientists are here from October to March. This is actually a new station, a prototype that they're leaving here for the winter. There are no winter stations on this island. The generator has been drained of fuel. Solar panels disconnected. Everything's been shut down. Feel how cold it is?"

Hamilton let out a breath of steam. "Icy."

"What do the stilts do?" Amy asked. She was stalling, looking around. Wondering why Dr. Jeff was here. She knew it wasn't for krill.

"The stilts are adjustable according to weather conditions, so they left it high for possible snowfall," Dr. Jeff said. "Take a look at the bulletin board; it's got some cool stuff on it. I just need to grab my research. They get up to some pretty fun stuff here . . . horror movie nights, costume nights, Popsicle contests, you name it."

With wary eyes on Dr. Jeff, they went to the wall and scanned the photos.

"Why Zimmer named that ship the *Titanic*, I don't know. It's cursed. Not that I want to stomp on his dreams. Everybody has crazy dreams, right? Mine is to get out of krill and into something that actually pays. You know what that is? Energy. You know who can help me do that?"

He opened the door, and the icy wind and snow swept in.

He grinned. "The Outcast. You should be able to see the boom from here."

They sprinted for the door, but it slammed shut in their faces. They heard the locks engage.

Hamilton yanked, but it didn't give. "That," he said, "was a serious miscalculation on our part."

They ran to the window. Amy heard the noise of a propeller. High in the gray sky, a helicopter was banking. They kept their eyes on it as it circled, looking for a place to land. It finally settled onto some shale. The pilot stayed on board.

It took a few minutes, but soon Dr. Jeff came from the direction of the beach, hurrying toward the copter.

Amy beat on the windows, even though she knew it was useless.

In just minutes, Dr. Jeff had climbed in the copter and flown away.

CHAPTER 34

The snow was now a whirling mass of white. It had taken no time at all for the three of them to feel extremely cold. Jumping jacks helped, but they couldn't keep it up forever. Well, Dan thought, maybe Ham could.

"Ian will know we came ashore," Amy declared. "He'll find us."

Nobody said what they were all thinking. The ship was scheduled to depart. Ian could assume they were still on board. He would be looking for them even as the ship sailed on. Even as the explosion happened.

They searched the pod, but it was cleared out of anything they could use as a battering ram against the door. The windows were unbreakable. There were no blankets or survival gear. There was no food. Ham picked up a chair and smashed it against the door. The structure didn't even shake.

"This place is built to withstand high winds, blizzards, and snow accumulation," Dan said. "I don't think it will break, even for a Tomas."

They gathered couch cushions and piled them in a corner, huddling together for warmth. Dan tried to remember the symptoms of hypothermia.

Shivering. Check.

Clumsiness. I just dropped binoculars on my foot.

Slurred speech. Not yet. But then again, I haven't said anything in five minutes.

Ham stood and began to run in place. "We're going to get out of here, okay? Let's just keep our blood moving. There's no such thing as 'can't' in the Holt universe!"

Amy began to jump up and down, beating her arms against her sides.

"You two look like nerds," Dan said. "Let me join you." He jumped up and down, beating his hands against his legs. His fingers felt cold inside his gloves. "Too bad we can't shake this place down to the ground."

"Wait a minute." Amy stopped jumping. "Didn't Jeff say that the stilts are adjustable?"

"Yes, so that they can accommodate snow accumulation," Dan said.

Hamilton stopped running. "That means hydraulics, right?"

"I guess. Why?"

"Because there will be controls inside the pod, that's why." Hamilton started to roam around the space, searching frantically. "Here's a control panel," he called. "It's got lift controls for the stilts. It will work without electricity! Gravity is on our side."

"But what good will that do?" Dan asked. "We'll just be closer to the ground and still won't be able to get out."

Ham glanced around the room. "Not if we torque it."

"What do you mean?"

"If we pile the cushions in a corner . . . and barricade ourselves . . . and do three legs at once. . . ."

"Exactly," Amy said, totally in tune with Ham's thinking. "We collapse three legs so the whole thing crashes down and torques at the same time. The stress on the corners . . ."

"Might snap it."

"But what about us?" Dan asked. "It would be like being in an elevator falling five stories. Not to mention when it cracks apart like an egg!"

"Do you have a better idea?" Amy asked. "We've got to get back to that ship!"

"Ready?"

"Ready."

Amy and Dan braced themselves behind a wall of cushions.

"One, two, THREE." Hamilton pressed the switches on the hydraulic lifts for supports 1, 2, 3, and then

dove into the cushion fortress as the modular structure began to tilt.

"Here we go!" he yelled.

Dan had only a moment to look at his sister's terri-
fied face, and they were falling, fast and hard, tilting
and sliding. He bounced hard against something and
shouted from the impact. The window was suddenly
in front of him, and he saw sky and then rushing
ground and snow.

The crash sent him flying, hands over his head. He
heard a horrible, wrenching *crack*. He tumbled again,
flying through the air and landing hard, his face
in snow.

Snow! He was outside!

He couldn't breathe. Was he hurt? He didn't know.
Gingerly, he rolled onto his back.

Pieces of blue wall lay splintered on the snow. The
modular base had cracked open and spilled them out.
Dan looked for Amy. He saw a spot of red on the snow.
It looked like blood.

"Amy!" He screamed the word, torn from his
lungs. He fought his way through snow and debris
toward her.

It was the red parka. She was lying flat, face to
the sky.

"Amy?" He tripped and stumbled and landed on
his knees. "Amy?"

Her eyes opened. "Sky," she said. "We made it."

"Are you okay?"

"I'm okay." She raised herself, wincing. "Hamilton?"

"WOO-HOO! RIDE OF A LIFETIME!" Hamilton stood on a slight rise, the broken pieces of the station around him.

"We've got to get"—Amy flipped over onto her hands and knees and struggled to her feet—"to the ship. We're only a half hour away from the blast!"

On shaky legs, they ran past the skeleton structures of the whaling station and the rusting tanks. The Zodiacs were still on the shore. They raced toward them.

But they were deflated, the knife slashes still evident.

Amy felt tears spring to her eyes. "Jeff disabled them. We'll never get out of here in time."

"There's no such thing as 'CAN'T' or 'NEVER' in the HOLT UNIVERSE!" Ham shouted.

"Oh, Ham, I know," Amy said. "But we can't cruise out of here on hope alone."

"No, dude." Ham took her head gently and turned it. "We're going to cruise on out of here on Ian's ZODIAC!"

CHAPTER 35

Ian rammed the boat up on the beach and leaped off, his bright yellow parka billowing behind him. Relief was evident on his face, but he held his body stiffly, as though he was trying not to hug someone or whoop with joy.

Instead he raised his chin and said, "Only for you would I ever put on this jacket."

"We're just glad you're here," Dan said. "You and your jacket."

"Cara got a message through to me. The ship—"

"Is going to explode in less than thirty minutes," Amy finished. "We know. Tagamayer rigged it. He just took off in a helicopter. We don't know how he did it, or how to stop it."

"Sammy sent a text about how to stabilize the fuel. Something about phenolic compounds and methyl esters and the oxidation stability of UVO."

"What does all that mean?"

"It means I broke into the ship's kitchen and stole four gallons of used canola oil," Ian said, gesturing to the Zodiac. "We've got to get it inside the fuel tank. It will gum up the valves, but the ship won't blow." He patted his pocket. "I managed to lift a key card from a crew member."

"So let's go," Amy said, starting toward the Zodiac.

"One second," Ian said. "I saw Alek Spasky aboard the ship."

"Are you sure?" Amy asked. "But why would he be there, too?"

"If I were running this operation, I'd have a backup, wouldn't you?" Ian said. "He's probably got a plan to disembark, but considering we have no time and there's a trained assassin running around, the odds are not in our favor. There's a strong possibility we won't make it. So . . . there's no reason for all of us to go. I just came here to make sure you were all right. I have emergency supplies in the Zodiac that I can leave with you. Cara knows where we are. Some of us can be rescued. All of us, in fact. Except for one."

Amy looked hard at Ian. She'd seen him step in front of a gun. He had the courage to face death.

But he couldn't sentence the rest of them along with him.

He couldn't order them. Couldn't bear to. And the chances of him doing it alone were so, so slim.

Dan shot a look at her. She understood him in an instant. They had to take the choice away from Ian.

Dan pushed past Ian and got in the Zodiac. Amy followed. Hamilton clambered in.

"Guys, I do think we should consider—" Ian started.

"Just push us off and get in the boat," Dan said. "It's time to go save the *Titanic*."

Ian pushed them off the beach and climbed in. Amy steered through the ice floes back toward the ship. They motored fast through the narrows and hit the open sea. Snow pelted their faces. Amy barely felt it. Every nerve was screaming to get back aboard that ship.

Hamilton looked like a bandit with a scarf pulled up to his eyes. Dan held on to the sides of the Zodiac, peering ahead, watching for the ship. She met Ian's eyes briefly. She knew he was torn up inside. The responsibility was killing him. She could see it.

Amy concentrated on weaving through the ice floes. A massive iceberg lay ahead and to their right. She saw the *Titanic II* emerge from the mist and snow.

And a metal spear whistled through the air and thudded into the side of the Zodiac.

CHAPTER 36

"Get DOWN!" Ian shouted, and they all ducked as another spear whistled past them and thudded into the opposite side of the boat.

Ian yanked out the spear. It had a ring in the middle. Cara had sent him a photograph. It was the same weapon that had killed Rollo Hardcastle.

Dan and Hamilton flattened themselves on the sides of the boat. Amy had slid down to the wood planks at the bottom, keeping her hand on the steering mechanism and her face forward. Her face was pale, her lips pressed together.

"There are air compartments in the boat!" Hamilton shouted. "We won't sink!"

Unless he shoots out too many compartments and they fill with water, Ian thought. *Too many to stay afloat.*

Just like the *Titanic.*

The bow was deflating as the boat bumped over the sea. Ian lifted his head to peer behind them, through the pelting snow.

Another Zodiac was chasing them down, its bow lifted with its speed. Ian could see Alek Spasky at the helm, steering with one hand. The other held something spinning. . . .

"DOWN!" Ian shouted.

Amy zigzagged to the left, and they jounced against the boat.

This time the spear punctured the boat just inches from Ian's head. He could hear the hiss of air as the cushion deflated.

Seconds later, another spear punctured the stern.

He was going to shoot out the compartments, one by one.

Alek must have a plan. Maybe he was supposed to leave on the same helicopter as Tagamayer. He wouldn't re-board the *Titanic II* now. He wouldn't want to blow up with the ship. He would sink them, and then watch the ship blow.

Because the Zodiac was sinking. It was dotted with spears and was low in the water, flabby and losing air by the second. Dan's face was grim, and Hamilton looked at the *Titanic II* as though he could physically tug it closer to them with his gaze.

Ian looked at the ice floes in the gray water. How long could one last in water this cold? Ian had read that experts estimated that some of the *Titanic* passengers had lasted twenty minutes in the ocean, but this water was even colder. And there were those predatory leopard seals that might make the experience even more unpleasant.

He thought of the victims of the first *Titanic* disaster, the shock of hitting that freezing water, the temperatures that shut down their body systems as they desperately tried to stay afloat. . . .

"We're going to make it!" he cried. "Just keep going!"

But they weren't going to make it. The massive iceberg was to their right, preventing Amy from escaping that way. Alek's boat was now to their left. Ian stared at the massive iceberg. Through a narrow tunnel in the ice he could see whirling snow on the other side. Up this close, he could see how the surface of the berg was fractured and uneven and contained shades of blue that were unearthly in their beauty. As he watched, a crack above widened and a chunk broke off to fall with a spectacular crash into the sea. He felt a jolt of fear. If they'd been closer, it would have sunk them.

Another spear thudded into the right side of the boat. Only three compartments were still inflated.

"DOWN!" Ian shouted, and another spear hit.

Amy turned the boat to the right and Ian glanced nervously at the iceberg. He could see fissures widening into cracks, and cracks widening into fractures. If Amy got any closer, they'd be in danger.

"Amy, I think the iceberg is calving!" he yelled. "Watch it!"

Amy glanced over, her eyes roaming over the berg. "I'm going to try something!" she yelled. Ian could hear the terror and desperation in her voice.

"Everybody . . . just hang on tight! Ian, tell me when Spasky spins the spear!"

Ian twisted, hanging on while keeping his gaze fixed on Alek. Alek dipped his hand down into the Zodiac, then Ian saw the glint of metal, spinning and gathering velocity. . . .

"NOW!" he yelled.

Amy yanked the steering at the last minute. The spear splashed into the gray water, and Hamilton cheered as the Zodiac surged to the right.

Ian lost his breath. Amy was steering straight for the iceberg!

The iceberg that was beginning to calve, the split now visible at the top as a chunk the size of a railroad car began to split off . . .

And tumble . . .

Chunks of ice rained down, and they covered their heads. The spray of snow blinded them, but Amy never let go of the tiller. Even over the engine they heard the massive cracking of the ice. The Zodiac zoomed into the ice cavern as the huge chunk of the berg crashed into the sea. Ice and snow splashed into the sea, and pieces as big as Ian's fist landed in the Zodiac.

"Hang on, we're going to get backwash!" Amy yelled.

The water moved as though a leviathan was beneath them, tossing them forward and bumping them against the craggy walls of the iceberg. They were well inside the iceberg now, and everything was gray and blue and showered with snow. More fissures appeared, cracks radiating down from the top.

The roaring of the engine and the ice mingled as they shot out of the tunnel while another massive chunk calved off the berg and crashed behind them.

They rode the rolling wave back to the *Titanic II*.

Hanging on to the side, Ian wiped the snow out of his eyes and swept the bay behind them. Alek was having trouble keeping the Zodiac floating in the backwash of the water. He tried to navigate past the huge railroad-car-size berg, and gave up. He turned the boat around and headed back toward Deception Island. Heading for the helicopter, Ian thought. The one that wasn't there.

Amy rounded the stern of the *Titanic II* and bumped the boat up against the platform.

"That was a little close," Hamilton said.

"It's about to get closer," Dan said. "Ten minutes until she blows. Run!"

CHAPTER 37

Titanic II, *Antarctica*

They skidded to a stop in front of the door marked
ENGINE ROOM CREW ONLY.

Ian swiped the panel and pushed open the door.
They found themselves in a small locker room. Hard
hats were piled in a box, and orange coveralls hung
on hooks. They each took a hard hat and put it on.

A crew member walked through the door. "What
are you kids doing down here?"

"We're meeting Mr. Zimmer for a tour," Amy said.
"He should be here any minute. We are super excited!"

"Get a look at the guts of the ship, eh? Don't forget
your earplugs." He pointed to a case. "And don't go in
there by yourselves!"

"Of course not," Amy promised, and waited obedi-
ently until he'd passed through the exit door before
grabbing earplugs and leading the way into the
engine room.

Immediately, they were hit with heat and noise. They were in the bulkhead of the ship. They walked out onto a catwalk that ran above and through massive machinery painted bright green. Everywhere they looked they saw a confusion of machines, gauges, pumps, pipes, and controls. Three stories of catwalks and ladders crisscrossed the space. Below them, a thick yellow shaft ran the length of the space.

"That looks like the prop shaft," Ham said, leaning in so they could hear him.

"Can you find the fuel tanks?" Amy asked, trying to keep the urgency in her voice tamped down.

Hamilton anxiously peered down into the guts of the ship. "There. Come on."

"We've got four minutes," Dan said.

They scrambled down a ladder to the lowest level of the engine room. A mechanic with his back to them was walking toward a staircase. They waited until he climbed up, their nerves taut and straining. Luckily, it was so noisy that no one could hear them, so they just had to move quickly and hope they weren't spotted.

Even through the earplugs, the noise of the machinery thudded against Amy's eardrums. She felt the engine power in her body, in her bones. Each heartbeat counted out the seconds.

They ran behind Hamilton to a massive metal tank. Ham climbed a small ladder to the top and unscrewed the valve.

He motioned, and Ian passed up the first gallon of oil. Ham poured it in, tossed the empty back down, and motioned for another.

The oil seemed to pour impossibly slowly.

Dan held up two fingers. Two minutes.

Ian pointed to a touch screen with several monitors. "Keep your eye on the pressure gauge. It's spiking, but it should go down once the oil mixes in."

The gauge was in the red. Amy watched as it edged farther into the DANGER zone.

Hamilton kept pouring.

The gauge stopped moving. The needle trembled.

Dan held up one finger.

Ham reached for the last gallon and poured in the oil in a steady stream.

He closed the valve and stood still, waiting.

The gauge began to sink back down into the green zone. Slowly. They watched it, their heartbeats hammering against their chests.

"It's at a normal level!" Ian cried. "HOORAY!"

He straightened his cuffs. "I mean, good show. I knew we could do it. Though Sammy wasn't one hundred percent sure it would work. Did I mention that?"

"No," Hamilton said. "Thanks for leaving that part out."

Amy smiled at Dan. Her legs felt weak.

"We did it," Dan said. "This *Titanic* won't sink."

CHAPTER 38

Ushuaia, Argentina

Jonah let out a whoop as the text came through.

"They made it. They saved the ship!"

Cara jumped up and threw her arms around him. They bumped hips in a dance.

They made it, they made it, they made it. . . .

Jonah's phone buzzed again and he ran for it.

"It's Nellie!"

IF WE DISAPPEAR ASK MABEL

WHO IS MABEL? Jonah tapped out.

SAVE MY KIDDOS

WHO IS MABEL, Jonah tapped again.

There was no response.

CHAPTER 39

Attleboro, Massachusetts

The Outcast smiled. At last he had the place to himself.

So little resistance from the rest of the Cahills, he mused. It was something of a surprise. He'd planned for it, of course, even looked forward to it, but no resistance came. That Kabra boy was weak. Pathetic. No wonder his father had disowned him.

Now they were happy, thinking that they'd bested him.

They would soon learn how wrong they were.

Let them race all over the world, let them try to beat him, and he would be right here. Right where he wanted to be.

It was lucky for him that the children had chosen to rebuild Grace's mansion almost as a complete replica of what she had. Of course they had made changes—that extra floor with the digital suite and the apartments for visiting Cahills—it would all have to go. He didn't want guests. He wanted solitude. And memories to fuel him.

He climbed the stairs to Grace's library. This room they had reproduced exactly, down to the molding and the windows and the fireplace surrounded by green tiles. He remembered it all well. The same window seats covered in deep green velvet, and it looked as though—yes, very nearly—they'd replaced almost every volume in the bookshelves.

Even the entire set of Shakespeare.

He ran his hand along the spine of *Much Ado About Nothing.*

Very funny, Grace. But I would have thought you would choose Macbeth. *Considering your penchant for blood.*

The hidden compartment slid out. So. The children replicated *everything.*

The safe was inside. It was fireproof, so it had survived.

And he still knew the combination.

He spun the dial and heard the clicks. The door opened and he reached inside.

He tossed aside the flat velvet box—priceless pearls didn't interest him. He withdrew a folder.

He took it over to the comfortable armchair by the window and began to leaf through the documents.

Oh, yes. Very interesting.

And just what he needed to destroy them.

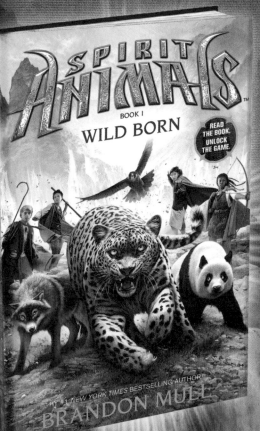

СВИДЕТЕЛЬСТВО О СМЕРТИ

ХАРТФОРД
фамилия

25
числа

1967

1967

ЗАСГ
гистрации

 Commonwealth of Massachusetts

City of Attleboro

№ 13334

CERTIFICATE OF DEATH

NAME Grace Madeleine Cahill AGE 78

DATE OF BIRTH December 24, 1929 DATE OF DEATH August 17, 2008

CITY OF DEATH Attleboro, MA

MARITAL STATUS Widowed

SEX Female

CAUSE OF DEATH Cancer

RECEIVED IN THE CITY/TOWN OF Attleboro

 CITY CLERK